LUCY ON THE WEST COAST

LUCY ON THE WEST COAST

AND OTHER LESBIAN SHORT FICTION

BY MARY BETH CASCHETTA

alyson
books

LOS ANGELES • NEW YORK

Manufactured in the United States of America.
Printed on acid-free paper.

This trade paperback is published by Alyson Publications Inc.,
P.O. Box 4371, Los Angeles, California 90078-4371.
Distribution in the United Kingdom by Turnaround Publisher Services Ltd.,
Unit 3 Olympia Trading Estate, Coburg Road, Wood Green,
London N22 6TZ, England.

First edition: October 1996
First paperback edition: October 1997

01 00 99 98 97   10 9 8 7 6 5 4 3 2 1

ISBN 1-55583-426-4

Library of Congress Cataloging-in-Publication Data
  Caschetta, Mary Beth.
    Lucy on the West Coast and other lesbian short fiction / by Mary Beth
  Caschetta. — 1st ed.
    ISBN 1-55583-374-8 (cloth); ISBN 1-55583-426-4 (paper)
    1. Lesbians—United States—Social life and customs—Fiction. I. Title.
  PS3553.A78976L83 1996
  813'.54—dc20   96-22489 CIP

For Susy

"I am a girl, so I do not get a gun."

—*Alice Walker*

Contents

Still Life

My mother returns today from town with a carful of chaise
lounges. This is not a good omen. Even my father, standing behind curtains, watching her back the car up the driveway,
shakes his head. He is already brewing a pot of coffee to wake
himself up, steady himself for the day's activity, which, like me,
he has been dreading all week.

"What is it?" I ask.

"Lawn furniture."

My mother whistles a happy tune, tossing and catching
her keys without interrupting the bounce in her step. Snapping
open the hatch of the Volvo, she pats the hood as if it were a
friendly cat.

I see them through the window: a dozen at least, stacked in a neat pile and brightly colored. From where I am standing inside the house, I can tell they are Scotch plaid and pastel, lightweight but durable, the sort that's meant to last.

The prospect makes me nervous.

My mother is not the kind to take receipts, a habit that fills the basement and crawl space of our attic. When a new fashion hits, there is always the question of what to do with the old decor, garage sales being decidedly out of the question. We are not that kind of people, she says.

Numbly I walk to the kitchen, hoping that whatever my mother is cooking up, whatever she is planning to do with all those lawn seats, will bounce off me rather than stick.

We are accustomed to odd behavior, but this is new. Recently our lives have become unmanageable. It is as if some invisible line has been crossed. When Eddie closed up his photo studio and moved back home, my mother frosted her hair and changed all the wallpaper. When Eddie battled night sweats long into the morning, she stood dead center in each of our rooms, so motionless, she could have grown moss. When finally she got down to the stripping and gluing, it was a cosmic game of stop and go—in and out of fevered activity and muscle-clenched trances—until she had repapered every wall in the house.

The weird part, the part that's hard to fathom, is that each new pattern is nearly identical to its predecessor. At most there is a shade or two of color difference, a tiny variation in the width of a stripe. Connections being what they are in my family—delicate and loosely strung—no one says a word.

We merely look the other way.

Things between me and Eddie are hard to explain. I tell myself this: Eddie is my brother, and yet he is not really my brother.

When he is being nice, we go places together and do things. I used to know all his friends. I used to stay over at his apartment in Rochester. Before getting sick, he lived in a neighborhood filled with old houses divided into dark apartments. Sometimes my mother refused to let me stay over with Eddie because of the upsets on his block. Drug busts and robberies. Once a guy on Oxford Street, two blocks from Eddie, was convicted of murdering the mail lady—tried to peel back her skin, they said. The first time Glen and I had sex was on Eddie's sofa. Eddie said it would be okay as long as Mom never found out.

The other way—the way he's not my brother—is complicated. When I was young, Eddie used to do things to me. Things I didn't understand at the time. He is seven years older than I am; I was five when it started, his sneaking into my room at night to kiss me on the lips and put his hands down my pajamas. During the day I was his pretend girlfriend; he bought me things in exchange for silence. I wouldn't have told, though. Besides, now that Eddie's sick, he leaves me alone.

I try to move on, pretending the past never happened, at least not to me.

The refurbished farmhouse where we live teeters on the edge of a small town called Irondequoit, a name handed down by Indians. There are remnants of their culture—tomahawks buried in people's backyards, oddly shaped stones prominently displayed in the town's museum—but not much else.

Our backyard has no tomahawks. It is a large sloping hill the size of a football field, with a steep drop-off into the lake, a kind of rocky cliff at the bottom. To hide this fact, my mother has built a wooden jetty. Like everything else, she designed it herself, obsessively, one summer, the year the Olympics were held in Lake Placid. The dark-stained planks jut out in neat rows, resembling the color of blood, and the dock extends so far out that a careful dive lands you in deep, cold water.

A person has to be careful because of the rocks. The day the dock was finished, my mother bought me and Eddie matching Olympic-style suits. She stood on the planks, grilling us until we dived like swans.

"Discipline!" she would bellow repeatedly, like someone swinging a punch.

Again and again we climbed up the ladder, gripping the edge of her sturdy new structure with our small white toes, throwing ourselves in the air. My mother liked the idea of graceful, winning children.

"Did you go for the gold?" my father would ask cheerfully at dinner.

Eddie always got a perfect ten.

Our address is miles away from everything. My parents, both of them teachers, have chosen this life of eccentricity and isolation. They are not country folk, they are not Indians—they are not even from this place, which is so far upstate, another few inches would make it Canada. My mother was born in Chicago, my father, Brooklyn, so there's no explaining.

They rarely make trips to the nearby cities like Toronto, across the lake, or, in the other direction, past the bay through the lonely wheat fields to Rochester, New York. Once in a while they take a drive out on Five-Mile Line Road, which leads to the middle of town. They maneuver their ten-year-old burgundy Volvo to an old parking lot behind a tiny post office, where they pick up mail-order packages from the catalogues they collect, or else park outside Hegedorn's to gather provisions. The few exchanges they have are with former students— grown-up men and women—who bag their groceries, deposit their checks, and talk incessantly about getting out, something they will never do. My parents sympathize as if they too are trapped.

The morning of the lawn chairs, my mother breezes into the kitchen, still high from her shopping.

"Sara," she barks, "help your father unload the wagon."

My father splashes coffee onto the kitchen table. My mother slips through the sliding glass door without so much as a second glance and out onto the back lawn, moving so quickly, my father doesn't have a chance to open his mouth. Not that he ever would.

She's a magician, my mother: able to suspend time.

Poised at the edge of the patio in her neatly pressed jeans, she clenches her chin in her hand and squints over the tiny half glasses perched on her nose. Nothing in her expression changes. Making a shadow over her brow, she points her face in the vague direction of Canada, planning something bizarre to take the edge off.

It used to be exciting to see what she would come up with, but after a while a person gets tired of the show.

By the time my father and I have pulled all the lounge chairs out of the wagon, brought them around to the lake side of the house, and carried them down the grassy slope, my mother is hard at work. Resigned to menial labor, we slump up the hill, back to our Saturday chores. Allied, my father and I are complicit misfits, shuffling our lives in neat little piles around hers.

In the kitchen my father heads for the cellar door, bumping down the stairs in his socks. I spend my Saturday afternoon doing dishes and finishing my homework at the kitchen table. I'm not the best student, but I do all right; mostly I lose focus. Anyway, I'm really waiting for Glen to call.

My mother hates Glen. She hates the way he slouches, the black under his fingernails. She hates how he will probably never amount to anything, never, if left to his own devices, go to college. She hates that Glen's mother owns a boutique that sells ladies' clothing, that Glen never had a father, that he doesn't act ashamed. Most of all, though, my mother hates that Glen is not dying of a mysterious disease.

Glen doesn't call very often, mostly when he's bored with fixing cars or when his friends aren't around. Sometimes he wants to have a date, which means sex. But even that isn't more than once a week. I call him to go to the movies downtown, but he doesn't call back. I've gotten myself in the habit of waiting.

By the end of the afternoon, my mother has created a constellation of patio furniture down by the lake. It's a strange construction, but almost mystical, I have to admit. Somehow she has transformed the whole backyard into a gigantic carnival of aluminum pipe and plastic weave, a sprawling universe in beach chairs. My mother believes that Lake Ontario will cure Eddie if he sits next to its glistening shore long enough. She has to believe that something will heal her firstborn, her only son.

Still, fate is finally tempting her to switch allegiances from Eddie to me. Even as she reminds all of us that Eddie was once on the front page of the *Democrat & Chronicle*, even as she continues to admire his good looks no matter how pale and sickly he grows, my mother is being tested. Still, it's not much of a choice. While she waits on him, pretending nothing has changed, my mother continues to hate one thing more than sickness: weakness, a code word she has for the female sex. That this includes herself does not lessen her contempt even a little.

When Eddie calls for us to help him out of the bath, my mother tells him about the chairs. She has arranged them in a healing pattern she copied out of a catalogue called "Coven."

Eddie scrubs his legs with a washcloth.

"A new chair every day," my mother says firmly.

Eddie is tall; in the tub he has to bend at the knee in order to fit. Though I am used to seeing his body without clothes on, I don't like to look. I study my sneakers.

"Every chair corresponds with the zodiac," my mother continues, searching his face.

"Amazing," Eddie says, as if he hates her.

The water laps around his ankles; we hear the faint hum of the radio from the basement where my father is listening to a ball game.

Eddie rinses, and my mother pulls the drain.

There is something else. It takes me a full minute before I realize what it is, and I try to pull my eyes away from the back of Eddie's neck, but I cannot: Scaling the base of his head to the midway point between his broad shoulders is a string of bumps the size of crab apples, sticking out like tiny doorknobs.

For a minute I consider the possibility that they are tumors from another infection. Then all at once I see how thin he is: These lumps are his bones, fragile and pointy, as if wooden hangers were stuck just under his skin.

Vertebrae, I remind myself.

I repeat the word to make it seem familiar, but everything looks different, separate and connected at the same time. Even my mother, bossy and small, seems like a stranger I've met only a few times. This is the bathroom, but there is no privacy. This is my mother, but she doesn't love me. This is my brother, but he is also someone else.

"What's the matter with you, Sara?" my mother is saying. "Get the towel."

I get a clean towel from the rack and hand it over, which breaks the spell, returning me to my body. My mother steps into the tub on Eddie's left side, while I support his right. She doesn't seem bothered by the sight of Eddie's wasting form or my participation in his nakedness. It seems as if I have always been in this situation, ever since I can remember. Everything feels heavy to me, even his hair, as I help her maneuver him to the toilet.

I concentrate on remembering that Eddie is my brother. I think of all the really nice things he has done for me, how he protected me from bullies. Bought me ice cream. Helped me with my algebra.

"Look at me," he used to demand at breakfast. "Why are you staring at your food like that?"

Sitting there on the toilet, he seems suddenly fragile, bent in an arc, surrounded by white porcelain. I stare at him, imagining an apology.

"Okay," he says to my mother, who picks up the wet towels and heads for the door.

Eddie demands his privacy. He insists on dressing himself.

I try to remember what it is I need to tell him.

"Get out," he says, and all my thoughts scatter like clouds.

The summer unreels more and more out of control, days cluttered with my mother's projects. One night at dinner she announces that she will not be returning to her job as a junior high school guidance counselor. She's decided to build an addition onto the kitchen, a glassed-in porch with a bathroom. She describes it in painfully technical details.

It is nearly September.

"This way Eddie won't have to bother with stairs."

"Well, there's an idea," my father says, because somebody has to say something.

Once, Eddie would have reached under the table and grabbed my hand, smirking and rolling his eyes. Now he picks at his chicken, not saying a word.

Labor Day my mother begins to draw up blueprints, price lumber. Eddie sits by the lake watching for boats. He indulges her silently, trying out new chairs, taking occasional photographs of the view. During her work breaks, she sits with him. I sneak up behind them, eavesdropping on what they say to each other when no one is around; I am sure it is something secret.

As I move into close range, I hear Eddie tell my mother he is feeling a little better; the chairs are starting to work. For the first time, I see that he is afraid. My mother, on the other hand, punches her hands on her hips, as if her work as a mother is finally done.

Once she begins a race against the weather, I linger near the house with my father. We all leave Eddie to himself down by the lake as we stare through kitchen windows, past the crowd of empty chaise lounges where he rests, over the boats that sit like a still life on Lake Ontario, out to a simple horizon, beyond which is Canada. Canada must be a pretty nice place, I think. A place where people don't die of bizarre diseases, where no one pretends a brother isn't a brother. Sometimes I think that's where we're looking when we stare off into space, toward that better country.

The Chase Pickin', where my mother takes me to help her pick out lumber, is a long, thin rectangular building fronted with potted ficus trees and located in the middle of town. Inside, the floors are buffed to a high polish. Mysterious objects glint from the walls. Neatly piled on shelves, gadgets of all sizes are squeezed into every crevice: coffeepots, can openers, rat pellets. The place is crawling with salesmen in powder-blue jackets. A sleek canister of butane gas catches my eye as I finger a display of matchsticks for the fireplace mantle. The soles of my mother's white tennis shoes squeak as we wheel our basket to the back of the store, trailed by women in more squeaky shoes who look and sound uncannily like my mother.

Our clerk, a former problem student with a lisp, has hunched shoulders and smiles nervously, keeping a constant eye on his digital watch, which is almost twice the size of his wrist.

"Mom," I say, after he's gone to check the stock out back.

It comes out more plaintively than I expected. A few ladies turn reflexively to see what's wrong. I move in closer to clarify my loyalty.

"I need to talk to you," I whisper.

"We're here to shop," my mother says sharply.

"I think something's wrong with me," I say. "Maybe I have what Eddie has."

I flirt with actually telling her.

"There's nothing wrong with you," she says, slowing her cart to eye me suspiciously. "You're fine."

"But, Mom, I don't feel very fine."

"Don't be ridiculous." She rolls the cart to a complete halt.

"Doesn't it kind of seem to you…?" I start, but I lose the rest of the sentence.

"I've been busy," my mother cuts me off, "in case you haven't noticed."

I recognize my mistake too late to take it back.

"Just stick with me, can you? For once in your life, just try, until Eddie gets better and moves back out on his own."

She delivers this sentence with a fevered pitch that makes me realize she is lying to herself. Her eyes dart around the store, unable to land on me.

The store grows dim, as if there's been an electrical surge in my brain. It's too much to consider she might already know.

The clerk pops up in our aisle just as my mother says crisply, "Buck up!" then turns to the boy who's breathing asthmatically at my back. To him she delivers a direct order: "We'll take the pine."

Sometimes our house gets so quiet, it's as if my father's not poised by the sliding glass door, waiting for coffee, and my mother's not hunched over the kitchen table, reading her architectural magazines and making notes. She tapes indecipherable drawings to the refrigerator door. At first I expect a message, perhaps an apology.

I peek over my father's shoulder. "What's it say?"

"It doesn't say anything," he answers. "It's the room."

His body is worn now, slouched into a question mark, as if so many years on the planet have caused him only confusion. A math teacher, the principal of a private school, my father has spent a lifetime convinced that two plus two equals four, but lately the equation is giving him trouble. His life, my mother's behavior, Eddie's illness—just about everything seems to elude him.

To pass the time, he takes up smoking. It's not much of a hobby—lying on a beat-up '50s-style sofa in the basement, practicing his sleight of hand, lighting one cigarette with the orange end of another, as if he might someday be able to compete with my mother's magic.

Other times I am convinced that we are all cosmically fixed to the same invisible point on the horizon, exactly over Eddie's head, where our eyes converge: Canada.

My father and I carry lumber, listening to my mother's plan for installing windows, so Eddie can continue to look out over the lake. The leaves have finally changed all their colors, threatening to fall away like chips of paint. My mother has been dreading this sign all summer; she is offended, as if this natural progression were some divine plan staged to annoy her.

Eddie is in his usual place, stationed in one of the chairs by the lake. Without thinking, I take a seat next to him, consumed with an idea that his apology is imminent. Blindly I believe that he is sorry, just as I believe that my mother will eventually have to surrender to nature's superior persistence; she will never finish the room on time. We're in the nervous, warm weeks of September, the start of a new school year, when any salvation is worth holding on to.

Chattering on about Glen and my classes, I sit with Eddie, watching for sailboats. I pretend that he is a stranger, someone I've just met on a bus or a train. I can tell it irritates him, but I don't stop.

"Maybe Glen and I will get married or something," I say, lying, testing the water.

"Why?" Eddie wants to know.

"I don't know. Something to do. Nothing ever happens around here."

He steals a look over his shoulder at our mother, who is busy sizing up the aluminum siding and sunning her legs at the same time.

"What do you think about that?" I say, waving to a pile of wood stacked up next to the house. "I mean, shouldn't someone do something?"

"Nothing to do," he says.

"Today she bought each of us a tool belt," I say nervously.

"Just shut up, Sara," he says, as if he is having a separate conversation that suddenly collides with the one I am having. "Why do you have to sound like her?"

"What?" My voice is shrill; it carries out over the lake.

"You sound just like her." He shakes his head. "Stuck—and ridiculous. And a liar."

I suddenly feel like a person who's been starving for an entire lifetime.

"I don't know what the truth is," I say, immediately recognizing that this is a lie.

Eddie just looks at me. Then suddenly he is staring. He hasn't looked at me in a long time, but I still recognize the signs of danger.

Slowly Eddie lifts his body from the seat, straining forward. I'm not sure what he means to do, but I rise with him, keeping my hands loosely at my sides in case he's going to fall or throw himself in the water or start back toward the house for his nap.

He does none of these things. Instead, he stands for a long time looking at the sky, then slowly bends over and picks up one of my mother's chaises. It is a green-and-pink pastel weave with a rocking-chair bottom. He walks to the edge of the neatly manicured lawn. Just before stepping onto the jetty, he throws it into the lake. I listen for the descent, wait for the splash. The effort and the waiting nearly knock my brother off his feet.

"Well?" he challenges.

Immediately and automatically I pick up a chair, walk to the edge, and toss it in the lake as easily as if it were a stone. It is exhilarating and frightening; it is also familiar. He smiles, grateful for my compliance, though he has never had any reason to expect otherwise.

I like the power of dismantling my mother's constellation, but the idea isn't mine, and that is part of the trap.

Eddie smiles again and takes three steps backward, reaching for a chair. This time he falls. I can hear my mother screaming (*Finally*, I think). But in my heart I know that nothing can stop Eddie. Ignoring her, he claws at a long blue chaise next to him, trying to fold it in half.

I continue, frenzied, throwing her chairs, one by one, into the lake. They float in the water like dead fish. Maybe they will float that way all the way to Canada, I think, watching the waves carry them out to sea.

Over my mother's shoulder, the last of the day's sun is reflected in all the windows of the house where Eddie and I grew up. She is nearly halfway down the yard by now. There is no noise from the open screens, but my father appears in the doorway. Everything feels slow-motion. I turn to where Eddie has collapsed in the long green grass, surprised by how calm I am.

"Help me," he says.

The water is cold as my body slides into it, a perfect dive. I stretch out one arm and then the other and feel like I am moving forward for the first time. I kick my legs against nothing but water, the small waves of my own movements carrying me forward. It is silent under the water. It is dark brown and alive with weeds and pebble-size fish that bump into me as I glide.

When my head finally breaks the surface, I can see Eddie sitting in the only remaining chair. My mother and father have helped him up, and now they are running toward me. They stop in their tracks where the length of the wooden jetty runs out. It is clear to me suddenly that they never learned to swim. They stand there, helpless, looking to one another for an answer. I hear my mother call something. My father joins her. Maybe it is my name, or maybe they are saying good-bye.

I watch them get smaller and smaller as I drift north.

If I swim through the night, I tell myself—even if I float on my back the whole way—I will reach Canada by morning.

Consecration

Every Saturday at Our Lady Queen of Martyrs Junior High, known throughout the Bronx for convening a cheerleading squad of beautiful Italian virgins, I was mesmerized. They mounted each other dutifully, bodies stiff as stepping stones, and climbed into formation to convince even the nuns that victory on earth was not all bad. Teresa-Marie, Kakhi Fondello, Elena Beth, Antoinette, and the three Marys—Ellen, Grace, and Jo: I was a slave to their synchronized routines, their rigid grace, losing myself completely as boys with bad skin dribbled past my vision.

Every year I barely made the squad, eking out the meager position of stand-in, an extra set of eyes for spotting lovely back flips, pretty but not pretty enough. On days when the real cheerleaders suffered twisted ankles, bad hair, and broken hearts, I was allowed to wear my uniform—a faded sweater and hand-stitched skirt made by someone's mother—and cheer, but only from the sidelines, not out on the court at halftime. Out of uniform, I sat in the bleachers looking after their jackets and lipstick, never allowed to mouth the words.

When no one was watching, they lifted me like a cross above their stalwart shoulders, toning their muscles, practicing their art after school. Sometimes they lost their footing, dashing me to the ground or catching me in midair, but every time they bent to pluck me anew from Our Lady's wooden floorboards, I escaped the misery of my caste: paper-nibbling boys, absurdly smart girls.

I knew, of course, that giving in to the world's temptation was sinful; I repented by holding my breath as those virgins sweetly pinned my ankles and gently tugged my wrists, hoisting me toward heaven. I could not help loving the feel of merciful angels holding me weightless in air, as if they might truly teach me to fly.

My mother found salvation through martyrdom and hardship, her saviors a congregation of God's civil servants, their hair in dowdy buns demonstrating a life of sacrifice.

At night I studied their pictures to ensure my place in heaven, still moved by their regretful faces: Mother Seaton, a matron from the Midwest; St. Dymphna, watchful over the nervous and mentally ill, her shrine at Gheel curing even the fidgety; Maria Faustina, the unsightly Secretary of Mercy; humble Clare of Assisi, foundress of a lowly order, Meager Bride of Christ; and withered, old St. Anne, my mother's favorite, Patroness of Housewives. I knew that when it really mattered, salvation belonged to the homely. Cheerleaders had shags and led us to glory, but they couldn't help in heaven; not even Jesus himself, I was sure, would understand my devotion. Lust was a burden; it was everywhere. I could smell it on my breath every time I said my prayers.

Before finding true love in the eighth grade, I allowed my cheerleaders to flatter me with cosmetics and remote stories of intrigue: kissing boys in the back of the auditorium where the nuns never went; stealing each other's dates and wardrobes and occasionally resorting to eye-scratching squabbles; falling in and out of infatuation with Father Charles, a young, handsome priest who taught biology. All the while, they continued to win shiny trophies for their acrobatic acumen, which I loaded on the back of the bus after every successful competition.

Friday nights we gathered in Kakhi Fondello's basement to discuss *our* new routines, bleach *our* unseemly mustaches, wax *our* hairy legs, compare *our* dreamy boyfriends. Kakhi, an olive-skinned beauty (real name: Mary Katherine), would look me straight in the eye as she handed me the tweezers, an act that somehow made me feel naked—and warm. She never seemed to notice that none of Our Lady's jocks actually belonged to me.

One day in the stale gymnasium while I was watching them create a stiff configuration I'd seen them perform a hundred times before, a dismaying realization overcame me: In or out of uniform, I looked like Kakhi and every other girl I wanted to kiss. Wanting cheerleaders equaled loving myself, a possibility as remote as the humble charity of my mother's saints. It was selfish and narcissistic to adore my own image in someone else's body, someone who wasn't even Jesus. According to my mother's long-suffering martyrs, self-love was not intended for females.

So in response I tried out for the soccer team, from which I was instantly cut. I experimented with facial hair, plucking my eyelashes and growing my eyebrows, and finally resorted to simple disguises to hide myself from even me: I'd pull my father's baseball caps down over my eyes, swaddle my small bust in blue Catholic cardigans, and wear tube socks everywhere I went, even cheerleading practice.

"Boys don't like jocks," my cheerleaders warned. "Especially when they're girls. You could go out with Eddie Fabini if you'd just try to be a little more feminine."

But I didn't want Eddie Fabini or any of his friends—tall, lanky tomcats who barely inhabited my peripheral vision. I found them strange and vaguely unpleasant to be near. Occasionally they attempted to win me over with their sweaty flirtation and milk-sour breath, but I was cagey and knew how to dodge. All Eddie had over me, as far as I could ascertain, was the ability to make the cheerleaders giggle and turn red whenever he cornered them in the hallway. Furtively I watched as he held the sticky hand of one after another of my beloveds.

Mutating my lust into envy, I soon returned to shaving my legs, seeking instruction on eyebrow plucking as I inspected the perfect half-moons of hair above their flashing eyes. If I couldn't lick a neck or finesse a kiss, I was at least going to steal a beauty tip. Almost sadly I noted my own transformation, wondering why the cheerleaders were losing their appeal.

Then one day, at the far end of an empty gymnasium, hours after school had let out, Nellie Tan, a husky new girl of no foreseeable consequence to cheerleaders, knelt down matter-of-factly on the basketball court and took six of the team's star players (boyfriends of cheerleaders) into her mouth, one after the other, an act that would have dethroned even the original Queen of Martyrs.

"It took her 44 minutes and 29 seconds," reported Mary Grace, fresh out of love and still stinging. Nellie Tan's talent, it turned out, had been recorded by Joey Massy, who accidentally turned on the scoreboard timer as he reached for the light switch. All at once, for their sordid connection to Nellie Tan, boys didn't seem so dumb.

The girls whose boyfriends weren't involved were first to push this major transgression through the complicated circuitry of after-hours gossip as if to see what it would look like out the other end.

"I heard she was the one who arranged the whole thing," Mary Ellen Mastrioanni said excitedly into my phone. One of the less popular cheerleaders, she nonetheless had an opinion on everything.

"You'd think these kinds of things would happen in the dark," I said.

"Oh, no, they like to be able to see," she said, "probably so they can believe it's really happening. I heard she never made a sound."

Somehow, the idea of her silence impressed me most.

"Teresa-Marie's boyfriend got on line twice!" Antoinette told me.

I worked the gossip over and over into a sizzle: those nervous boys waiting on line expectantly as if to receive the Holy Ghost, that mysterious eighth-grader bowing before sinners with an accepting tongue, blessed and wicked all at once.

"They formed a line!?" I wanted more details. "Was she on her knees the whole time? Do you think it made her gag?"

Not since Lourdes had I considered such mysteries. All this from a girl whose arrival at Queen of Martyrs had gone completely unheralded.

When I looked up Nellie Tan's picture in the yearbook to fuel my vision, I was disappointed to find it missing among the pages, leaving my urgent fantasies to buzz around my head like a swarm of greedy flies. Puberty, it appeared, had chosen that very moment to take hold, opening me up like an overripe melon. As I tossed and turned in my sheets, I couldn't help but worry about the implications: Nellie Tan had crossed an invisible line that only the beautiful, who created and maintained it, could see. She was trespassing in a world that didn't belong to her, unwittingly overturning the whole caste system at Our Lady Queen of Martyrs with the simple twist of her lips.

I knew what lay ahead: a bundle of trouble. I wanted to protect her as a reward for her bravery. All night long I lay in my bed watching the world transform into sex.

The next morning I squeezed myself into the doorway of Martyrs, dodging the drama of popular girls and their scuffling, denying boyfriends. All the way up and down the corridors, emotions ran hot—even the nuns seemed startled by the news—but I had other worries: What if she didn't show up? What if I never got a chance to see her in the flesh? What if there really had been no such bold girl, the stories of lust a cruel, cruel trick?

I had been oblivious to Nellie Tan's arrival, a miracle of courage and creativity dumped on my doorstep—someone who'd thought of one thing even the cheerleaders hadn't yet dreamed up. Nervously I waited in the brisk morning air until the third bell, twisting my hair into spirals. Freshly bleached and waxed from an evening of reconfirmed femininity, I glowed from my fevered dreams.

When at last I spotted her—head slung low, shoulders hunched high, thick brown loafers kicking out in front and stumbling behind—my life came sharply into focus. Nellie was my perfect match: the robber to my cop, the Indian to my cowboy, the butch to my femme, bowing to pleasure basketball players just as I bore the weight of cheerleaders. Our acts of submission were the same—feeble attempts to belong to a world in which we were both unexplained and inexplicable.

I searched her gait for shame or pride, cunning or humiliation, but found nothing, no visible trace. Her indifference enthralled me, making my desire quicken.

"Hi," I said, dropping off the school's front step.

She glared at me, a wild dog about to snarl.

Shy but hungry, I persisted. "I wouldn't go in there if I were you," I said earnestly. "Until things die down, we should probably go somewhere else today."

Unimpressed by the offer, she shifted her slim hips almost imperceptibly behind the itchy wool of her plaid blue uniform. She stood thick-limbed and calm, each of her fingers thicker than two of mine.

"I'm really not one of them," I said in the wake of her silence. "I barely made the squad this year."

"Yeah, right." Her voice was thrillingly husky; I felt deprived never to have heard it before. It was going to be a considerable task to convince her of my virtuous intentions, I could tell. "They're planning terrible things," I said, desperate to be of service. "Ambushes, scarlet spray paint, pudding in your locker."

She stepped to the side. I stepped with her.

"Listen," I said, "you don't seem to get how serious this is."

"I'm not afraid of a stupid bunch of cheerleaders."

Seriously underestimating the meanness of Italian girls, Nellie Tan may have found her salvation in basketball players, but I could picture them standing in front of Kakhi's locker, littering the hallways with their denials and insults. None of them would ever look her in the eye again. As Nellie Tan shrugged her broad shoulders, brushing past me into the school, I felt a kind of pain I'd never felt before.

"No ugly girl is going to ruin our lives," vowed Kakhi Fondello. It didn't take her long to mobilize the others.

By third period, Mary Jo Rizzo, a cheerleader with a troubled family, had stolen into the principal's office. We convened in the girls' locker room to see the inky blue carbon copies Mary Jo had slid off the desk of one of the nuns and was now standing there fingering.

"Failing grades, a transfer student from Lower Manhattan." She announced only the important facts, as if they explained everything.

Elena Beth sat on the edge of the bench, holding her arms across her chest.

"How could Joey have done something so disgusting with a perfect stranger?" she cried.

Comforting her, Antoinette said, "Maybe he really just watched."

"It was that slut," Elena Beth cried. "She doesn't belong here. Why doesn't she go back to wherever she came from?"

"I didn't even know there was a new girl," I said innocently. My faith in cheerleaders continued to wane.

"That's not the point," Teresa-Marie said, nudging me aside.

"She came in November from public school, lives in the neighborhood now," Mary Jo continued, cupping her hand over a stolen cigarette; her brother, we all knew, had been in and out of reform school. "Her father came from China."

"Figures," the other Marys said.

"Slut," a few of us murmured.

"Her mother's American."

"What about the boys?" I asked, afraid of where the conversation was going.

"Probation tomorrow," Mary Jo answered; there was no break in her police-report tone. She produced six pink slips from her pocketbook, evidence that the suitable penance for unsanctioned blow jobs in the school gymnasium was two days at home.

"But there were six of them," I said.

"What's that supposed to mean?" Kakhi wanted to know. For Catholic girls, sisterhood was a foreign notion.

"Well, maybe they convinced her, maybe she was forced."

"Forced?" Kakhi sputtered. "Since when does the school slut need to be forced?"

When I started to speak, Kakhi bore her sharp eyes down on me. "Never?" I guessed.

"That's right, never," Kakhi said.

"Never," a few of the others echoed, as if saying catechism.

A natural leader in a weary world plagued by too many references to virgins and girls named Mary, Kakhi detailed plans for stuffing Nellie Tan's bra in the hand dryer (I suspected she wore undershirts) and bombing her with water balloons. As we dispersed into the narrow paint-peeled hallways of Our Lady Queen of Martyrs, I resolved to keep my mouth shut, possessed of a new admiration for my mother's saints standing bravely against worldly evil and wrongful deeds. To the left side of my lagging courage, a painful stabbing nudged me one step further from the world of cheerleaders.

"Distraction," announced Sister Mary Stephen, a zealot who taught us both Euclid and the Bible in alternating semesters. To her, math problems were as much God's weaponry as faith; at the school assemblies she prayed like a Mack truck, evoking all sorts of violent imagery, bludgeoning temptation and whipping the devil. In a way I liked her best, though this did not ease the shock of being under her thumb.

Clasping a brambly hand onto my shoulder, she stood smugly next to my desk. Through her touch I could feel her excitement at catching a red-handed sinner: me. It ran through my body like a bolt of electricity.

Usually I handled classes easily; a good student, I doodled my way from English to Bible to French class, listening half-heartedly as I figured out life's more difficult problems. It was the prayer assemblies that made me nervous; I often blanked out on the confusing archaic words of the Apostle's Creed, even the Lord's Prayer.

The day I first laid eyes on Nellie Tan, however, my mind went cloudy, missing the signs of Sister Mary Stephen sniffing out sinners. Seated in the front row, I was an easy target.

Sister Mary Stephen leaned dramatically over my little desk to review the diagram I had been etching in my notebook. A sketchy drawing of events in the gym, down to the last detail, the scoreboard timer with only a few minutes left to go. At the end of the line, I drew myself, a foot shorter than basketball players, my heart darkly outlined inside my chest, my body lumpy in a cheerleader's uniform. I watched devoutly as the color drained from the sister's already pale cheeks.

The priests preferred violence, twisting their rings palmside to knock on the heads of the distracted and rude with ornate rubies or onyx that hinted obscenely at material wealth. The nuns were more wily, reading our private notes out loud to the class, loving to watch us die a thousand public deaths.

As Sister Mary Stephen inspected the boarders of my paper, where I had scribbled the name of my beloved, I held my breath as she followed the looping script so furiously, her eyes appeared to be spinning out of her head. I waited for punishment, the sound of her voice announcing my sins; instead, she got on her knees, pulling me down with her.

"Hurry, child," she whispered hoarsely. "Pray to the Immaculate Heart of Mary. Repeat after me."

Like in a fire drill, I scrambled to my feet, then sank to my knees, the blood rushing to the top of my head.

"I, Elizabeth Ann," Sister Mary Stephen said, pronouncing my name loudly to the front of the room where we wrote theorems and performed mathematical feats.

"I, Elizabeth Ann," I echoed softly.

"A faithless sinner…"

"A faithless sinner…"

"Renew and ratify today in thy hands."

"Renew and ratify today in thy hands."

My voice came low and hollow in the decrepit little room. I could hear the sound of my classmates' breathing as they twisted in their seats to watch.

"O Immaculate Mother, the vows of my Baptism…"

"O Immaculate Mother, the vows of my Baptism…"

I told myself that Nellie Tan was worth suffering for. She had been brave; so would I be. To my surprise, this obvious opportunity for martyrdom incited me further; I lifted my voice to match the conviction I had previously witnessed only in nuns.

"I renounce forever Satan, his pomps and works," continued Sister Mary Stephen fervently. When we got to the part about the pleasure and sacrifice, I picked up speed, closing my eyes and listening intently to the beautiful words until I'd caught up with Sister Mary Stephen. Together we headed for a hair-raising finish:

"In the presence of all the heavenly court, I choose thee, this day, for my mistress, I deliver and consecrate to thee, as thy slave, my body and soul, my goods, both interior and exterior, and even the value of all my actions, past, present and future; leaving to thee the entire and full right of disposing of me, and all that

belongs to me, without exception, according to thy good pleasure, for the greater glory of God, in all time and in eternity forever and ever. Amen."

Bewildered, the other students watched, slack-jawed, as Sister Mary Stephen and I, glowing with internal fires, recovered our breath, the bell finally ringing at last. We arose in unison, like secret lovers, each confident of what we had learned, fortified in a bond by the Act of Consecration.

After class in the hallway, Teresa-Marie caught up with me: "What was that all about?"

"I don't know," I lied. "I guess the nuns are edgy today."

"I guess so," she said as I melted away to study hall.

For exactly three months Nellie Tan suffered my devotion without response, occasionally berating me into doing what she wanted, until it seemed that no other way of wearing my hair, copying down homework, eating lunch, or even dialing the phone had ever existed. Bad things continued to happen to her: anonymous letters, illegal tackles in intramural softball, threatening phone calls late into the night. By the spring her father had moved the family to Chicago, where it was rumored he'd been transferred. I never got to say good-bye. One day, in the spring of 1972, she was simply gone.

I knew about the world's strange dyads—good and evil, women and men, blacks and whites, Democrats and Republicans. Yet it took me a long time before I understood what Nellie Tan had offered. Although the women's movement stepped off my end of the subway line that summer, just as I was turning thirteen, its clarifying messages were just a distant buzz for another decade, light-years away from my restricted universe.

Later I would come to know them all: professional femmes who'd cut you to shreds; soft butches who wanted your whole hand; watery "one size fits all" girls residing somewhere in the middle, denying they belonged to either camp. I even received beauty tips from a couple of ex-cheerleaders who ultimately left me standing in the rain as they went off with women who looked like boys or men they'd decided to marry.

But for a very short time, in the spring of 1972, before Nellie Tan or I could know who or what we would become, I held that husky girl to the pavement, my eyes burning. For more weeks than I thought possible, I walked beside her under a flat, waxy sky, from which, like a miracle, the crisp night always descended to offer us relief. I no longer even thought about cheerleaders: I'd found a place in the world alongside Nellie Tan, a girl who was indifferent to my allegiance, who barely tolerated my adoration.

Ignorant of how much a heart could ache, I was happy to walk by her side in silent prayer the entire way home.

Nuclear Family

As Kennedy recalled it, the photographs of Fran appeared a few months after Kennedy's dad had packed up and moved two streets down the block with an abundantly cheerful stranger named Joyce. Now the pictures were a regular feature on the mantel, barely worth a mention: her mother and Fran peering out over the living room furniture; best childhood friends at the World's Fair; licking ice cream; petting Ohio cattle for somebody's camera, probably Pop-pop's.

At first they didn't seem like dangerous girls. But, scrutinizing the position of Fran's broad hand on her mother's slim shoulder, Kennedy couldn't be sure. In the photo of Fran diapering Davey in the field of some nameless hippie festival,

Fran seemed to be gazing meaningfully into the empty air; in the third, she stood off center, with her arms around Grandma and Pop-pop, probably in Sarasota, where they had retired a few years ago and, shortly after, died. The silver frames alone provided evidence of Fran's long-standing family status, but they didn't explain her sudden reappearance or prominence in Kennedy's life.

It was winter when Kennedy's father met Joyce at the Wal-Mart, just about the time Kennedy's mother discovered the small knots under her armpit, moving them aside the way an accountant might finger the beads of an abacus. When they didn't go away, she paid a little more attention, discovering two—three if she counted the sore spot closing in on her left breast. At the time, Kennedy's mother ran a private therapy practice out of the basement for mildly depressed people— nothing extensive, mostly run-of-the-mill marital problems or simple boredom. That particular day, while Joyce was selling Kennedy's father a deluxe snowblower, Kennedy's mother canceled the rest of her appointments and sat in the kitchen drinking coffee, trying to figure out how to tell her family. But as Kennedy later figured, the cancer had arrived too late: Joyce had already closed the deal.

As if to add insult to injury, Fran herself materialized, arriving just a week after the appearance of her photographs. Just like that she was standing on the front porch, tall and blond, all her things stashed in a camping pack, as if she'd stepped out of a postcard from Europe.

"In the '60s, before you were born, everybody lived together in a collective," Kennedy's mother had explained. "Not just families, but everybody, together in one house."

"This isn't the '60s," said Davey, Kennedy's little brother.

Kennedy's mother pressed at Davey's cowlick, trying to be playful. He waited for a more appropriate explanation.

"Well, thanks to your father, I need help paying the rent."

Davey shrugged: "Why don't you just take the alimony money?"

Usually, at moments like this, their mother would make some comment about "the Reagan generation," but for the time being, a sigh was about all she could muster. Anyway, everyone knew about their mother's principles, so Kennedy was glad to skip it altogether.

Three years later (the summer Davey almost got killed), all of it—their father's taking off down the block with a sales-clerk, their mother's cancer, Fran's arrival—seemed like an exhausting dream, the kind that lingers long after you've awakened until something more disturbing can take its place. In fact, most of Kennedy's past appeared this way, particularly since she'd started fainting. No one knew what to make of her blackouts, though Kennedy figured that hunger probably contributed. She sat on the front porch thinking about it, about everything, wondering how stupid a person could be.

Fran had been living with them for three years now, and still nobody knew who she really was.

For a while Kennedy told people that Fran was a cousin of theirs who was living with them while looking for a job. But their corner of Cedar Rapids was small: Within weeks every-one knew that Fran had found employment gainful enough to enable her to get her own place. Kennedy's classmates reg-ularly reported new siblings who had been pulled into the world by Fran's capable hands in the special maternity hospi-tal at the edge of town where she'd been hired as head nurse.

Lately the more serious question of Fran's role in the fam-ily was coming up in conversations—tedious discussions dri-ven by Kennedy's mother. Cancer had spread to other parts of her body now, prompting a flurry of activity and doctors, which got people to thinking about what might happen to Kennedy and Davey should their mother really die this time. One thing was certain: Kennedy did not want to go live down the street with Joyce and her dad, especially now that there was a baby. It was slowly starting to dawn on everyone that Fran was their only option.

Kennedy was counting on Davey, her ten-year-old brother, to explain the whole thing to her.

In the meantime summer had gotten weird: Her father was smiling again, drinking highballs, hovering close by when Kennedy and Davey came to visit; the doctors were talking about getting the new cancer before it got out of hand; and Kennedy, for some unknown and embarrassing reason, had begun to faint in public, confounding even the pediatrician.

At each of Davey's Little League games, they arrived in their respective cars: Kennedy's dad in his Mercedes, straight from ChemCo in a suit and tie; Joyce and the new baby in a shiny green Honda, parcels from shopping loaded in the trunk; Kennedy's mother and Fran in a rusty old pickup truck, from work and a doctor's appointment.

It was mortifying.

"Love is blind," her mother blurted out.

On the way home she always brought the pickup to a complete stop at the corner in front of Kennedy's father's house because, as she said, the traffic sign told her to do so— she wasn't fooling anyone. The house where Joyce and Kennedy's father lived was nearly transparent, with windows on every side, all the way to the backyard where Kennedy's father was planting a Japanese rock garden, his latest obsession.

"Blind and lacking a college degree," her mother muttered to no one in particular.

No one laughed at any of Kennedy's mother's jokes about Joyce. Except Fran.

Sometimes Kennedy hated Fran. She hated the way she looked, with her big Midwestern face, her dimples, and her tall freckled forehead. She hated her straight blond hair and her big gapped-tooth grin. Kennedy's hair was thick and ropy, unlike Fran's baby-fine, shiny bob. She also hated the way Fran stood around, her expression as vast and welcoming as an open country road, her hands continually tucked in the back of her corduroy shorts, a sign of optimism. It was altogether creepy for someone to be so nice.

Whenever anybody mentioned Kennedy's father, Fran would stand stupidly aside, good-hearted and well-intentioned. When Joyce's name was spoken or the new baby's, Fran would screw her mouth into a sympathetic shape and eye Kennedy's mother. She was an encouraging presence as they shuffled around the grocery store together in halter tops, Kennedy's mother's breast conspicuously missing, like an odd item dropped accidentally from the shopping cart. Kennedy refused to be seen in public with them; she'd even started walking home from Davey's ball games through the woods behind the school. Her mother sported floppy hats with big sloping rims or borrowed baseball caps, wearing them bill-side back, as if no one in Iowa knew what was going on.

Now all of their lives were displayed like one of those stupid bumper stickers, announcing to anyone with eyes what was nobody's business in the first place: Her mother had had a mastectomy and was living with a strange woman, a childhood friend, whatever that meant. Her father had run off with a salesclerk from the Wal-Mart, who had become pregnant and had a baby before the divorce was even final. Her little brother was a freak who could easily graduate high school before passing the fifth grade. And Kennedy had suddenly become the focus of everyone's attention by reeling over backward at inopportune moments.

In short, things were falling apart.

"If you're so smart," Kennedy planned to ask Davey, "then who's Fran?"

Davey *was* smart; he knew entire solar systems by heart, had at his disposal words that even adults never used. Summers, when he wasn't in Little League, he spent at the MENSA Club of Iowa. He was particularly good at calculating the likelihood of abnormal occurrences, which he would announce to strangers in the supermarket or mall. "Hey, lady," he'd say to some nice-looking mother in a sundress, "given the heat, the number in that bin, the reduced-sale sign, and the lack of rainfall, which is pretty much killing off the crops, chances are pretty slim that those melons aren't already spoiled. Prices should be going up, not down.

"You're better off buying frozen," he'd add wisely.

Davey was also obsessed with barometrics and, in fact, took to predicting the weather before every Little League game—so accurately that the coaches found him indispensable, despite his clumsiness. This season, of course, the midlands hadn't seen a drop of rain, so there was little reason for Mr. Abernathy to call Davey, but athletes seemed loyal to their rituals, Kennedy noticed.

Once, after her brother had spent the whole year standing on the front porch, at the same hour every evening, as if taking a mental photograph of what appeared to everyone else to be nothing, they decided to take him to the doctor to make sure he wasn't autistic. Kennedy's mother had been reading everything she could get her hands on about autistic children and idiots savants. They all watched from the kitchen window—her father still with them then—while Kennedy's mother absently pulled at her eyebrow hairs until they were a mere memory on her face. It turned out that Davey was taking eye measurements to determine the precise dimensions of nightfall over the span of a calendar year. By the time he was nine, he had made projections for the hour of sunset for the entire following year.

"You wouldn't believe the mistakes they make in these things," he'd exclaim, perusing the new *Farmer's Almanac.*

"Freak," Kennedy said over her untouched breakfast.

"Kennedy," her mother scolded, shaking her head ever so slightly.

"Davey, honey," Kennedy's mother said, reaching over the kitchen table to gently smooth his hair, "Mommy was really worried about you. Did you know that? Maybe next time you can let us know when you're conducting an experiment. Okay, honey?"

"Well," Davey said sincerely, "maybe next time you'll ask."

He never meant offense. A slave to logic and all its principles, he simply expected the same of others, miscalculating the limitations of most people's intelligence. It was his most tragic flaw, wanting so badly to be understood by a world as rational and methodical as he was, a world that didn't exist.

Dunking his spoon back in the sugary bowl of cereal, he grimaced, a tuft of hair flaring up on his head like a spray of water from the garden hose. Kennedy felt both disdainful and sorry at the sight of his deep disappointment.

Their mother only laughed. "I will ask you next time," she said, smiling. "Probably I will."

Kennedy could just ask her mother outright about Fran, she supposed. Her mother was now humming softly in the laundry room, making the noises of someone still recovering from being sick, someone stuck in temporary slow motion. But the idea of asking directly scared Kennedy: She wasn't sure she wanted to know. Instead, she counted: yellow jackets; heat lightning; scorched leaves on the trees, which were coiled like fists against an arid sky. She counted: twelve saltines she'd eaten since Monday; twice this summer she'd fainted; three times since Sunday she and Davey had seen her father and Joyce, including Davey's baseball scrimmage; seventeen weeks since there'd been rain.

Shifting in her chair, she fingered five wicker marks on the back of her thigh, measured ten frayed strings hanging off her cutoff jeans, counted twenty-four little plastic water bottles from a box. Once a day they were allowed to flush. It all added up to August—humid and still during the longest drought in the history of Iowa—and only three weeks away from the start of Kennedy's first year in high school.

"I don't like it," Kennedy told her mother, who had finally emerged from the house.

The screen door barely made a sound as her mother stepped out into the late afternoon, a slow, airy yawn softly pinching it shut. Standing with a laundry basket in one arm, Kennedy's mother looked confused, as if she had been expelled from the house not of her own volition, her pale skin seeming exposed, as if it might pucker in the heat.

"I'm open to other suggestions," her mother said softly.

Coming to life again, she let her free hand rest lightly for a minute on Kennedy's shoulder. "It's just that I think Fran has been like another mother to you guys."

Kennedy shrugged, sticky under her mother's touch. *This is what it's like to die,* she thought, the air blistering all the way through her.

Kennedy's mother waded barefoot onto the front lawn, past waves of burnt yellow grass. Holding the bundle of damp laundry close to her hip, she felt her way carefully out to the midway point in the yard—a clothesline strung between two crooked birch trees—then set to work, deftly handling the wooden pins that pinched the edges of Fran's white uniforms,

Davey's pajamas, and two freshly bleached white sheets. They hung on the line like ghosts, as if they themselves represented the new family her mother desperately wanted to keep. Perhaps Joyce, just down the street, was hanging out the ghosts of Kennedy's other family; she imagined tiny white jumpsuits and fresh cloth diapers that never seemed to stain. The thought of the two competing families made Kennedy's skin feel prickly, as if her body might lift up off the sticky porch seat and dissolve into the impending dusk like a layer of Davey's predictable darkness.

The stench of Cedar Rapids was sharp this summer, lasting even into the evening. Quaker Oats, located just down the road, churned out vats of cereals, alternately syrupy and oat-smelling, which were mechanically herded into cardboard boxes. The odor of the factory, mingled with the unyielding heat, was even more poignant this year in the absence of rain. Kennedy felt as if a large unbathed dog were constantly panting bad breath in her face.

"It's too weird," she told her mother. "Fran isn't even related to us. Besides, Davey did the calculations. It's not like you're going to die soon."

Kennedy's mother smiled. "Gee, thanks."

She was petite, almost tiny, a fact that Kennedy used to admire but now resented, as it seemed to make her appear to be only steps away from the inevitable. Kennedy resembled her father, who was large-boned and awkward.

"You know what I mean," Kennedy said, rolling her eyes.

"Let's talk about this later, shall we?" her mother suggested. "I'd like to have it figured out before we see Dad and Joyce at the game tomorrow, but there's no sense beating a dead horse."

Kennedy winced at the mention of Joyce's name in the same sentence as *dead horse*. "That woman," as Kennedy preferred to think of Joyce, was always trying to put the new baby on Kennedy's lap. All Kennedy had to do was think of how the little neck connected to the melon-shaped head, and she felt sick to her stomach. The doughy, meaningless weight of her half sister, perched on her thighs, repulsed her nearly to gagging. Trying to keep her arms tight, in case the baby caved in or fell over, she stopped herself from thinking about the place where (as Davey liked to describe it) the baby's skull was still busy knitting itself together.

Kennedy knew the trouble with her mother had really started before Fran ever showed up. It all began when the lumps turned out to be cancer and Kennedy's mother refused radiation. The doctors scowled, emphasizing her foolishness. Kennedy's father stood around or paced awkwardly in his business suit, pleading with her.

"But what if you die?" He was practically in tears.

"Tell me something, Charlie," said Kennedy's mother, "do you or do you not remember when there were bigger problems than just whether or not we were going to die tomorrow? For Christ's sake, we were always going to die tomorrow. Remember Vietnam and the civil rights movement? Wasn't the whole point then that we were ready to die for something larger than ourselves?"

"I remember. But, Joan, that was then."

Kennedy's parents had met during a civil rights march, naming their firstborn after a president they still mourned.

Kennedy's mother started a therapy practice at a time when women didn't do such things, sending Kennedy's father to get his graduate degree in chemical engineering so he could work directly against the formation of more-advanced weaponry like Agent Orange. Instead, Kennedy's father ended up working for a chemical engineering company that produced advanced plastic tubing. Kennedy's parents maintained that he was working to make recycling more tidy in order to save the planet, but the lie was wearing thin.

Kennedy's mother started to become unreasonable.

"You are definitely not the man I married, Charlie," she would say.

Leave it to Kennedy's mother, Kennedy thought, to annoy even the sympathetic, smiling nurses in their crisp uniforms as well as the stately, reasonable representatives from the local cancer society. These latter were handsome Iowa ladies who came around with attaché cases to speak soft reason into Kennedy's mother's ear. The nurses had already alerted everyone in town to Kennedy's mother's unorthodox ways, so the cancer ladies came armed and ready. They handed her little pinkish-tan bags of jelly, explaining in intricate detail that the sensible thing to do was to cover up the missing places. They talked about expressing a new line, a new femininity, as if Kennedy's mother were shopping for bathing suits. They might as well have saved their breath.

Davey followed the breast ladies around the hospital, seeking data so he could calculate the likelihood of the prostheses' leaking, in case his mother decided to be reasonable. Dressed in skirts with tightly cinched belts, the breast ladies listened to Davey's questions; whenever any of them actually bumped into Kennedy's mother walking through the halls, they smiled quickly and looked away. Kennedy tended to side with them on this. Embarrassing.

When the cancer started to spread, a discovery that was made a short time after Kennedy's father deserted them, Fran arrived to take up his role as principal adviser. After many whispered discussions behind closed doors, Kennedy's mother finally agreed to undergo chemotherapy, a decision she blamed on Fran.

"I should never have let a member of the medical establishment into my house," she said, laughing. "Next thing you know, I'll be buying stock in the pharmaceutical industry."

Fran accepted her victory with a quiet smile.

Begrudgingly Kennedy had to acknowledge that, at least for the moment, some kind of sanity had been restored. She long ago had stopped trying to convince her mother to stay out of the sun, to sit in dark corners with comforting books, to surrender gracefully and quietly to cancer the way other mothers did. Her mother was making a scene out of dying, as if it were 1974, rather than a decade later, as if the world were evil and the government a conspiracy and even the air you breathed a poisonous capitalist plot. Her mother acted as if it were selfish to complain about whatever fate handed you, since there were always others less fortunate. Somehow her mother had managed to resist the philosophy of the '80s.

Sometimes she imagined that her mother's militant philosophy was responsible for her father's leaving: Maybe he'd changed his views and was afraid to tell her, maybe he knew in his heart that her obsession with women's lib and breastless appearances in public would lead to only more problems. Kennedy could see her surrendering all sorts of limbs, accepting her fate like the day's weather report, bravely asserting that there were more important matters to occupy her thoughts. Currently she was gathering evidence of a local spill from the Genet Nuclear Plant, news of which had been covered up when it happened a few years ago, except for the initial emergency broadcast system alarm that went out over the radio. Kennedy's mother wrote letters to everyone: She believed that the spill had caused her cancer, and she had located other women in similar straits who believed the same thing.

She'd already narrowed her therapy practice, releasing dozens of people who sided with Kennedy's father and Joyce.

When Kennedy's father delivered the news of his affair and his intentions to leave, she could have made him feel guilty, but instead she just said, "You do what you need to do—whatever makes you feel important."

Maybe, if Kennedy weren't careful, her mother would let her go too.

Now her mother's condition was not getting any better; since chemotherapy, things were touch and go. Kennedy was not pleased to admit that maybe Fran's adopting them was not such a bad idea. Maybe it only seemed half-baked because of the way her mother had blurted it out one morning after Fran had left for work—like an obscene joke.

It was true that Kennedy didn't want to live with her father and Joyce and the new baby. She didn't want to spend dinnertime hearing about his stupid rocks, imported from glaciers around the world, or the state of plastics in America. She didn't even care if she never saw him again, even if, more often than not, she agreed with him that Fran and her mother took things too far.

In general, Kennedy prided herself on being balanced, detailed, and reserved. She always ate just enough; with her mother in and out of doctors' offices and Fran at work all day, it was relatively easy to slip by a few missed meals. Sleeping late took care of any scrutiny missing breakfast might provoke. Unbuttered toast or a piece of fruit taken on her way out the door were easy to dispose of in the dump site at the end of their block.

She despised the smell of everything edible. Naked pickles lying next to a sandwich made her queasy, the smell assaulting her like something left to rot in the hot sun for days. She could not stand runny eggs, whether sunny-side up or down. She even hated the very look of potato chips, how each one would lie on the plate like burnt shells of a June bug.

Sometimes she stood with the refrigerator open, observing the Saran Wrap–encased odor-free packages, the plastic containers, and the neat rows of jars.

"What are you doing?" Fran said, coming up behind her.

"Nothing." She shut the refrigerator door so quickly, the tiny light left a neon imprint behind her eyes.

"It's a good idea, actually," Fran said, trying to make up for sneaking up on her. "I'd go for the freezer, though. It's cooler."

Trust Fran to think only of something innocent, like trying to keep cool on a hot day.

"Good idea," Kennedy said, escaping to the front porch.

Dinner was the trickiest. There were too many variables: Her mother or Fran, Joyce and her father—even Davey—seemed to pay attention to what and how much she ate. At her father's house, Joyce, who was an aerobics freak, made low-cholesterol, low-calorie meals that didn't remind Kennedy of anything rotten. Still, she knew it wasn't good to like the tasteless meals too much. The need for more food, once she got started, was sometimes a surprising temptation.

Sometimes she convinced her mother that she had ballet lessons or soccer practice; those nights she'd skip dinner altogether, climbing through the backwoods and making her way to the school yard. She would lie down in the quiet, burnt-out playing fields or sit on the hill watching the new sprinkler system water her father's rock garden, wasteful in the drought.

This new baby is so much better than your other children, Kennedy imagined his new wife saying.

Her father looked like one of those guys in the TV commercials who play with adorable kids, trying to look natural while selling fertilizer or house paint. He was tall and mildly handsome, with dirty-blond hair that was starting to thin.

What other children? her father would answer, even though he knew in his heart of hearts that he had a perfectly good daughter and a more than perfectly above-average son just around the corner, not two minutes away.

Kennedy had once witnessed a girl in her science class sprinkling scouring powder on a half-eaten doughnut, wrapping it up in a paper towel, and shoving it to the bottom of the garbage can so she wouldn't eat any more of it. Kennedy kept track of which girls sat tight-lipped in the cafeteria, standing at their lockers a thin tangle of bone and disappearing one by one before the twelfth grade. Kennedy had heard rumors about the places they could send a girl, where disgusting amounts of liquid food were forced through a yellow tube right down her throat. She saw a clear distinction between the stupid, starving girls and herself. They were fools, and they broke her first rule: Desperation is out of the question. Kennedy wasn't like them; she would never get caught.

Unwittingly she had stayed friends with a tenth-grader named Sara-Jane Anshaw, who had been a chubby girl in junior high school, the kind who gobbled down her cafeteria pizza and french fries and asked if she could have the rest of yours. By accident Kennedy discovered Sara-Jane, now a cheerleader, involved in the whole messy business of throwing up her food.

"I never thought people like you existed," Sara-Jane said to Kennedy one afternoon after school at McDonald's.

"What do you mean?" Kennedy asked.

"Well, you never eat very much," she said. "You always have the Oriental chicken salad without dressing, or you just drink a diet Coke."

"So?"

"Well, it's just so easy to eat three cheeseburgers and then throw them back up," Sara-Jane said, pointing over her shoulder to the ladies' room. "Why would anyone go to the trouble of dieting?"

Kennedy didn't bother explaining that, for her, not eating had nothing to do with dieting.

She stopped talking to Sara-Jane altogether, turning her head when they passed in the hallway as if they hadn't been friends since the second grade. A bewildered Sara-Jane left a couple of notes in curly blue handwriting in Kennedy's locker. SEE YOU AT LUNCH???? they always closed.

But Kennedy never sat with her in the cafeteria again. She didn't need anything—not a normal family who all lived together in the same house; not a stupid girlfriend who ate like a horse and barfed in a dirty McDonald's bathroom; certainly not turkey sandwiches, asparagus, french fries, or even steak on the grill.

The fainting spells, the most recent irritating attempt on the part of Kennedy's unruly body to betray her, stopped when she came up with a plan of eating saltine crackers, five every two hours, and drinking enormous amounts of water from the little bottles Fran replaced every evening on her way home from work. All Kennedy had to do was keep her stomach busy, and she could make it through the heat of the day without a blackout.

On Fridays she rewarded herself with one McDonald's cheeseburger, one hot apple pie, and one diet Coke—miraculously, the usual food rules did not apply to this meal, which she could actually enjoy. Friday was the night she stayed in with Davey—who ate one Big Mac, two regular hamburgers, one large order of fries, two hot apple pies, and a chocolate shake—while Fran and her mother went out to dinner at the Red Lobster and then a movie. Sometimes Kennedy felt hungover the next morning, filled with real hunger pangs and dreams of wrongful culinary luxuries. To stave off hunger, she meditated, imagining stones, conjuring up the shapes and varieties you might find on a beach near the ocean. Though Iowa is landlocked, Kennedy had swum in saltwater lakes and could make the leap in her imagination. On more difficult days, usually Saturdays, she ate as if her stomach were already full, imagining the saltines as slices of granite.

Sara-Jane's phone calls still came in sporadically, but Kennedy never returned them.

"You should have seen how your mother and I fought when we were your age," Fran said, chuckling.

Kennedy rolled her eyes. She couldn't bear another story about the Bobbsey Twins; everything always ended up with "happily best friends ever after."

"C'mon, Ken," her mother nudged, "don't be a fair-weather friend. Call Sara-Jane back."

Kennedy didn't know what her mother was talking about. Iowa had been in a drought for months; the weather was anything but fair.

Fran's red pickup finally pulled into the driveway like a dirty red rip in the evening, rupturing the dream Kennedy had slipped into while her mother was hanging out the laundry. Davey, still dressed in his baseball uniform—No. 9—rammed his shoulder against the passenger door, releasing himself from the old junker. Fran stepped out of the truck, still in her nursing uniform and white Tootsie Roll-bottom nurse's shoes.

"We're home," she called to Kennedy's mother.

Duh. Kennedy rubbed her eyes and watched Davey do a strange little dance all the way up the front walk.

"Hi," he said.

"Hi, dope." She didn't want him to think she'd been waiting for him.

"What're you doin'?"

"Nothing," she said. "Did you actually play this time?"

"Nope," Davey answered. "But I figure that since Little League requires every player to play at least once per season—including scrimmages, practices, and real games—they have to put me in tomorrow."

He sat on the step and started pounding his cleats on the porch until tufts of dry powdered dirt lifted into the air.

"Last game," he said, "unless we win, which we won't. The odds are 100 to 11 against it."

In the meantime, Fran had walked out to the middle of the lawn to help Kennedy's mother finish the laundry, which seemed to be taking an extremely long time. Fran took Kennedy's mother's arm and helped her to the front stoop, holding the car keys and empty basket in her free hand. It hadn't occurred to Kennedy that her mother might actually need some help.

"What do you say we all go to Red Lobster tonight?" Fran suggested.

"McDonald's," Davey whined.

Kennedy's mother looked relieved. Maybe she didn't really want them around.

"Wash your face," Fran said, "and you can come with us to the drive-through."

"Only if I can drive," Davey said.

Kennedy's mother had long since stopped trying to get Kennedy to go anywhere with them, deciding Kennedy had a phobia of moving vehicles.

"While Davey gets ready, I'd like us to try to reach a family agreement," her mother said, trying to catch Kennedy's eye. "It's about Fran's adopting you two."

It wasn't much cooler in the house. Davey squatted in the doorway, pulling off his socks and pants, as Fran stood above him with clean shorts and his sneakers tucked under her arm.

"Not this again," Kennedy said, punching her fist into her cheek as she sat on the carpeted steps leading upstairs.

"Think about it, Kennedy," her mother said. "Fran's practically another mother anyway."

"Hardly," Davey said, but then he quickly looked up at Fran and flashed her a grin. "More like an aunt."

Fran stood there, good-natured as always.

"Well, it appears that, much to my chagrin, I'm not going to be around forever. We have to make plans."

Fran chose this precise moment to disappear into her own bedroom to change her clothes. Kennedy could hear the shower being turned on.

"Of course, if your father contests," Kennedy's mother added cautiously, "it might mean that you'll both have to testify in court."

"Testify?" Kennedy said. "To what?"

Her mother pursed her lips and scanned the room. Kennedy realized she was looking for Fran.

Her mother's bones jutted out under the seersucker shorts and matching halter top. A bandanna was stretched from one of her ears to the other so as to cover up the soft tufts of hair on her head. During the months she had been undergoing chemo treatments, she had grown to resemble a delicate bird, Kennedy thought, a bird that had flown smack-dab into their sliding glass door out back. She wondered how her mother could seem so perpetually hopeful.

"I guess you'd have to tell the judge that you two would rather stay here with Fran and me than go live with your father and Joyce."

"Isn't there something else we can do?" Davey asked.

"This is not a movie," Kennedy's mother said, exasperated. "Our options are limited."

"You're not going to die tomorrow."

"No," their mother was trying to recover her patience, "but isn't it good to have a backup plan?"

"Not if it isn't going to work." Davey stood up and slipped into his shirt.

"Don't talk to your mother that way," Fran said, appearing in a pair of corduroy cutoffs, a damp washcloth in her hand. Her hair, which was wet, was slicked down and parted in the middle. She wore a short-sleeved shirt tucked in under a heavy brown belt that perfectly matched her sandals.

"What way?" Davey said.

He held his arms in the air as if for a stickup. Fran had to work around them to get the washcloth near his ears.

"All I'm saying is," Davey said, "we're better off just packing up and leaving town to a place that Dad and Joyce don't know about. Then, if you die, we can just go on living like always, with Fran."

"That's against the law," Kennedy's mother said.

Fran tucked Davey's dirty baseball jersey into his clean shorts, pointing to his untied shoelaces.

"Davey," Kennedy's mother said, "why don't you change into some real clothes?"

He wore his uniform religiously, every single day. Kennedy eyed her mother suspiciously; surely she knew better than to start on that old rant.

"Look," Davey said in a grown-up voice, "all I'm saying is, you'll never win a court case like that, as long as Dad is alive. He's the biological parent. Besides the fact that he abandoned us, he's got more right to us than Fran does."

"Shut up!" Kennedy said, catching everyone off-guard. "If you're such a genius, why don't you think of something?"

Davey's eyes filled with tears.

"It's okay, honey," Kennedy's mother said, having managed

to get up and put her arms around Davey. "We don't have to worry about it now. I'm not going anywhere. I'm right here."

She rested her chin on Davey's head and looked over at Kennedy. "I'm not going anywhere," she repeated.

Kennedy felt as if her mother were holding her too, even though she was clear across the room. Fran was studying her freshly bathed feet.

Under Fran's bed Kennedy found a box of old photos and some college annuals, which, together, detailed a life, one far beyond Kennedy's grasp. She waited for them to come back with dinner, wishing she hadn't yelled at Davey, especially since she was increasingly going to have to count on him.

In the family room she turned on the TV to warm it up for Davey's favorite Friday-night summer lineup. Flopping down on the sofa, she studied a photograph from the yearbook: her mother and Fran standing outside the dorm, dressed for field hockey practice. Except for the short haircuts, she liked the way they looked. She leafed through the pages searching for other pictures of Fran.

She didn't hear them drive up, but when Fran tooted the horn before taking off again, Kennedy looked up to see Davey bouncing in, a half-eaten hamburger tight in his grip.

"What are they—nuts?" Kennedy said; she'd been saving the question up all day, waiting to get him alone.

"No, dummy," Davey said, tossing himself down on the sofa next to her, a greasy hamburger wrapper stuck to his arm. "They're lesbians."

The day of the big game, Joyce, Kennedy's father, and the baby in its stroller sat on the bleachers several feet from Kennedy's mother and Fran. Kennedy arrived on foot, drugged by the heat; she had gotten out of bed at 11 to find a note from her mother fastened to the refrigerator with a magnet. It said: SEE YOU AT THE BALL PARK! MOM AND FRAN

She'd been hungrier than usual but decided to get by without breakfast. Now, eyeing her parents sitting there like resentful bookends, Kennedy could tell she'd made a mistake; her stomach hurt. Luckily, she spotted Sara-Jane, waving so furiously that the pearl nail polish she'd been picking off her fingers was flaking into the air. Kennedy headed toward the middle row of the bleachers where Sara-Jane sat beside her happily married mother and father. Sara-Jane's little sister played on Davey's team—the only girl in the league. The star of the Thirsty Red Dogs with more hits than anyone else, she was their starting pitcher.

Sara-Jane's mother smiled. "Well, hello there, stranger."

"Hi, Mrs. Anshaw," Kennedy answered back, nodding to Sara-Jane and taking the empty seat beside her.

"Looks like Davey's going to get his big chance," Mr. Anshaw said, pointing his chin toward Davey, who was trying to catch Kennedy's eye.

When Kennedy gave a brief flick of her wrist, a half wave, her little brother's mouth widened into a grin. Kennedy was grateful that the Anshaws were looking at her instead of scanning the stadium for her parents, who were firmly ensconced in their separate places in the bleachers.

The Thirsty Red Dogs were getting creamed. It was the fourth inning before they finally let Davey in the game. Kennedy could hear Fran's hoarse cheers above those of her mother and father; there was no sound from Joyce. After a brief and humiliating turn at bat, whiffing the ball in vain three times, Davey returned to his usual seat on the bench. He didn't seem to notice the groans and remarks from the crowd, his teammates, or his teammates' parents; he simply took out his notepad and began to write, a strange little smile on his face.

At the end of the inning, Kennedy's mother made her way slowly and carefully to the top of the bleachers, every step like torture. Kennedy could feel even her father's eyes clocking her movements, just to be sure.

Mr. Anshaw stood, offering his arm. "How are you feeling today, Joanie?"

"A million bucks, Pete," she said, smiling, before turning to Kennedy to add, "May I speak with you, sweetheart?"

"Sure," Kennedy said.

Reluctantly Kennedy followed her mother to the top row. She felt nervous, watching her mother walk ahead of her so cautiously, as if the slightest breeze might knock her off the edge of the bleachers. Of course, the day was motionless, dry as a dollar bill.

It seemed suddenly to Kennedy that the drought might go on forever, seamlessly. Something bad was in the air. Her stomach turned over again; she felt light-headed.

"Nice to see Sara-Jane and you back together again, like normal," her mother said.

"Whatever." Kennedy watched the Thirsty Red Dogs getting ready to man the field. Davey headed toward third. She let herself feel a twinge of excitement. "Look," she said, pointing in Davey's direction.

"Cross your fingers," Kennedy's mother said.

Ace Laundromat's Dirty Devils were ahead by so many points that it seemed Davey might see some action.

"Kennedy, there's something I need to tell you," her mother said. "It's about Fran."

Kennedy tried not to look down at her sneakers.

"You need to know what's going on," her mother said, as if Kennedy had spoken.

"What is it?" Kennedy squinted the sun out of her eyes.

"I'm in love, that's what," her mother said.

"You're in love?" Kennedy's mind began to race through all the options: Kennedy's biology teacher, Sara-Jane's father, even her mother's oncologist, who wasn't very handsome but seemed respectable. Maybe things weren't going to turn out so badly after all.

The batter was up, spitting gum and obscenities; he seemed older than the others. Kennedy's father was laughing with some of the other parents. She noticed the rise and fall of his shoulders, the preppie yellow polo shirt Joyce liked. Maybe her mother had fallen back in love with her father.

"Not Dad?" Kennedy said hopefully.

Kennedy's mother's eyes filled up with tears. The first pitch whizzed below their line of vision and popped up off the batter's swing. As if in a dream, Kennedy watched the ball head straight for Davey, who was holding his mitt in front of his face, blocking his view of the ball.

"Sweetheart," Kennedy's mother said, oblivious to the play, "I'm in love with Fran."

Kennedy was almost certain Davey wouldn't catch the ball, but it made a confident slapping sound, landing squarely in his mitt. Everyone was cheering loudly.

"Did you hear me, Kennedy?" her mother was saying. "Do you understand?"

Just as it was sinking in that Davey had caught the ball, Kennedy realized that the batter, in his zeal to get on base, had let go of the bat, letting it fly like a bullet right toward Davey's head. Kennedy's little brother, her only guide in life, a hopeless freak who whiffed at beautiful pitches, stood grinning, his foot on the base, eyes closed apparently in prayer.

Despite herself, Kennedy began to scream.

Coach Abernathy and Sara-Jane's little sister joined in; then everyone was screaming, their words coming slow and heavy. Only Kennedy's mother, who was turned toward Kennedy, didn't realize what was happening, that Kennedy wasn't screaming at her words. No one moved an inch, as the thoughts turned soft and gooey in Kennedy's brain.

Abruptly her mother turned, then rose, making her way down the bleachers. Kennedy's father and Fran leapt out of their seats in unison toward Davey. Before Kennedy could see whether they would reach him in time, darkness crowded in.

When Kennedy opened her eyes, the first thing she saw was an expansive afternoon sky, so blue and clean that it brought tears to her eyes. In a minute she sat up, rubbing her neck. No one was standing around her, fanning her with hot air, assaulting her cheek with soft, urgent slaps—she was completely alone. Her legs wobbly from her unwitting backward dive, she got to her knees, her eyes eventually focusing on empty Coke cans and candy wrappers. Through the splintery wooden rows of the bleachers, she could see that people had descended on the field like a pack of rabid dogs.

She was gingerly approaching third base when Sara-Jane's mother pulled her into a smothering embrace, grazing the lump on the back of Kennedy's head.

"Don't look, honey," Mrs. Anshaw crooned. "Your mom and dad are with him. It's bloody."

Kennedy stood stiff, strangely comforted by the shadow of motherly love, even if it wasn't her own mother. Surrendering to the sensation, she heard the sound of sirens fill the air.

"Here they come," cried the woman Kennedy now thought of as her mother's lesbian. Fran stood, poised, between the huge, bright hospital hallway and the stale rectangular room. Kennedy's little brother, stretched out on a gurney and wrapped in a papery hospital-issue gown, was returning from a second set of X rays, the men in white shirts and shoes rattling him closer and closer toward the room. It seemed like days had passed since Kennedy's father, her mother, and Fran had watched them wheel Davey away.

"The chances of that happening were a million to one," her little brother had blurted out as the attending physician examined him, trying to stop the flow of blood.

"Head wounds are always bleeders," someone said.

The doctor took Davey's comment as a good sign, but Kennedy knew that a coherent Davey would never be so imprecise.

"Maybe he won't be smart anymore," Kennedy whispered. Her mother ignored her.

Kennedy's attention was drawn to the orderlies, whose necks were thick and adorned with shiny gold chains. A metal taste stung the back of her teeth when she remembered their spicy aftershave. Unlike in the cancer ward, the nurses here seemed unfamiliar, almost curt.

"We can't tell you anything more than we know," one of them had told Fran soon after Davey had been sent up from Emergency. "So please stop asking."

Kennedy's father spent his time either staring out the door or disappearing down the hallway, his hands tucked under his armpits as if he were sizing up a golf course. When he reappeared to check up on Kennedy, he seemed friendly, though dwarfed by the oversize door. In fact, the whole scale of the room seemed lopsided, ludicrously out of proportion. Kennedy stared out the window at the parched landscape.

She could imagine her father wandering the halls, swimming like a salmon against a tide of nurses in white, an endless stream of people visiting the sick. In the cancer ward her father would probably remain equally unscathed by the

patients with their colorless webs of hair, striking his custom-
ary stance, hands in his pockets, ignoring them, busy with
periodic trips to the pay phone to call Joyce. In the cancer
ward, where Kennedy's mother was a regular, some patients
seemed healthy, as if at any moment they might throw on
their jeans and head for the door. Her father was just the type
to be confused by this appearance, striking up an innocent
hallway conversation with someone in remission, slapping the
stranger on the back, and cracking a joke about the morgue.

While Kennedy's mother stood around telling the nurses
how hard it was to keep everyone safe these days, Fran sought
out Davey's doctor to make sure he wasn't going to suffer any
brain damage.

In the meantime, Kennedy saw herself: a spiritless figure,
alone in the sixth-floor hospital room, a dark spot of fear in
her center like a stone. As if examining an X ray, she saw her
own loosely bound shoulders and wrists, the thick fibers of
her long hair, the hard, pearl shape of the stone in the center
of all her bones. She tried to imagine herself in the parking
lot, freed from Emergency, then in the pit of her father's
sunken Japanese rock garden, where there had been no rain
for months. From that distance she was almost invisible.

Davey's head was bandaged like a mummy. His eyelids
appeared to be flapping around as if he couldn't quite manage
to wake up.

"Davey?" Kennedy's mother called, trying to pull herself
together. "Can you hear me?"

As if he had been sitting in the backseat of the car and
couldn't hear her over the loud radio, Davey finally said,
"Yeah, Mom?" Kennedy rolled her eyes.

"How do you feel, honey? Are you all right?"

"I feel fine, Mom," he said loudly. A freak even in a crisis.

Kennedy's father stood on the opposite side of the bed

from Kennedy's mother. Each of them held a hand, as if trying to keep Davey from floating away. "Do you know what happened, Davey?"

"Sure, Dad," Davey said. "I got beaned in the head with a baseball bat."

"Why is everyone whispering? And why is Davey yelling?" Kennedy was exasperated. "Open your eyes, dummy."

Davey obeyed.

"Hi, Fran," he said, addressing the first face he saw.

Fran pulled out a hand from beneath her crossed arms and waved three fingers.

"Does she have to be here?" Kennedy's father said.

"Yes, she does," said Kennedy's mother.

In the thick silence Kennedy pictured a nuclear bomb going off.

Out on the playing field, before they'd managed to get a completely unconscious Davey into the ambulance, she'd held her little brother's limp hand, watching the driver fasten him to a gurney. All Kennedy had felt was a vague chill: Anger, happiness, fear, and sadness were things of the past. Her head was spinning as her mother and father climbed into the back of the van with the paramedics and drove away. Joyce took off without a word to anybody, probably to put the baby down for its nap, probably upset that Kennedy's father had insisted on riding with her mother and Davey to the hospital.

Kennedy slid into the passenger seat of the red pickup, Fran at the wheel. They rode in silence past three stoplights.

"He's going to be awake when we get there, Kennedy," Fran finally said. "It's just a cut above the ear. Heads always bleed like that. It's the first thing you learn in nursing school."

Kennedy buckled her seat belt.

"He's going to be just fine, you'll see. And, Kennedy...

nobody has to adopt anybody."

Kennedy turned from the fogged-up window, surprised.

Fran glanced at her.

"Your mother's going to be fine too. Her blood work looks good. By the time the cancer comes back, you'll be in college, maybe even graduated."

Fran tossed a pack of cigarettes on the dashboard in front of Kennedy.

"This is just a starter pack," she said. "Camel Lights, my old brand; you'll have to experiment to find your own."

She lifted her blond eyebrows above the Ray-Ban glasses. "Listen, starving yourself is a bad adolescent vice: It'll screw up your period and kill you if you're not careful—which I notice you are."

Kennedy could feel the skin on the back of her neck beginning to tingle.

"Smoking'll make you feel just as bad as starving yourself," she continued, "and you can quit before you go on the pill. Your lungs will renew, and you probably won't put yourself at any more risk than you already are."

The air conditioner pumped its mist onto the cellophane wrapper of Fran's cigarettes.

"I know you're not getting a lot of the things you need right now—we get the message. We'll try harder. But, Kennedy, everyone needs food."

To keep the tears back, Kennedy thought about the hospital parking lot: She remembered the first time she'd had to help her mother navigate all those yellow lines and jigsaw markings, with Davey finally talking them through the maze; they'd arrived a half-hour late for the very first oncology appointment in what seemed a subsequent lifetime filled with them. That was after Kennedy's father, but before Fran. She marveled that they'd ever found their way. Now, as Fran slipped effortlessly past the confusing signs and the jangle of color-coded arrows, Kennedy realized how familiar it was. They'd already arrived.

As Fran predicted, Davey was set to be released in the morning. Kennedy's father insisted that Kennedy stay at his house overnight. She didn't have much choice; Fran and her mother were camping out beside Davey's bed, and she didn't want to be alone.

Waiting for dinner was awkward. Usually Joyce took Kennedy and Davey to the Florida room, and they all watched *Oprah* until Kennedy's father got home from work. Tonight no one felt like television. Everything had an edge.

"My mother's name was Piggy," Joyce was saying; Kennedy lost track of why. She sat on a bench, watching Joyce make tofu and soba noodles. The baby was playing in her pen.

"Really?" Kennedy's father said. "I didn't know that."

He was mixing drinks for himself and Joyce at the counter. Kennedy didn't remember her father drinking. Joyce, she noticed, however, could really tie one on.

"Everyone in Atlanta is named for an animal," Joyce said.

"Little chicken?" guessed Kennedy's father.

Joyce howled.

"Kitten, right?" Kennedy said. "They called you Kitten."

Joyce was genuinely surprised. "How did you know that?"

"Wild guess."

"Ken," her father said softly, a warning.

"Sometimes I think she's the smart one in the family," Joyce said. She gave a sharp, winking smile. "Smarter even than the little genius with the bad eye for baseballs."

The baby cooed. Its name was Ariel, a candy name.

"C'mon, Ken," her father said, grabbing his highball glass and pulling the sliding glass door open. "Let me show you around my garden." And to Joyce: "Be right back, hon."

"Take your time," she said, not sounding like she meant it.

The Kirishma azalea was deep pink, its little flowers growing in a cluster. "Native Japanese," her father said, trying to impress. "Over here by these sandstone boulders I've planted rhododendron. You can't see them yet."

He had rocks of every sort, imported from all over the world: sandstone, cherry limestone, serpentine, volcanic breccia. The tiny pebbles underneath Kennedy's sneakers made her step uncertain; the bright pink bushes hurt her eyes. She was glad the sun was finally going down and that Davey's darkness was finally taking over the terrible day.

Her father drained the remains of his cocktail. "What do you think?"

"I think Mom's a lesbian," she said. She couldn't help herself. The rocks made her hungry; she wished she could eat a peanut butter sandwich.

"Oh," he said. "Well, yes, I suppose she is. She didn't used to be, but she is now."

"Maybe she wouldn't have become one if you hadn't left." Kennedy pulled a few flowers off a branch and let them fall to the ground.

"I don't know, Ken," he said. "Millions of women in this country are left by their husbands, and they don't turn out to be lesbians."

Kennedy would have to check the statistics with Davey.

"There's nothing I can do about it, Ken," he said grimly. "Is there?"

Kennedy watched Joyce's reflection through the dark glass of the house. A film came over the window when she strained the soba noodles, as if she were in a sauna.

"I guess when Mom dies," Kennedy said finally, "we'll go live with Fran."

"I guess so," her father said quietly.

Kennedy leaned into a breeze, wondering if she was imagining things; it smelled like rain.

Joyce opened the sliding door. "Soup's on," she said.

Making his way through the dark rock garden to the kitchen in his new house, Kennedy's father flipped on the outdoor floodlights. The night was warm and mostly still; a few clouds had gathered over Kennedy's head.

Joyce reappeared with a salad bowl in her hand.

"C'mon, darling, let's eat." She ducked back in, her voice trailing behind. "Looks like rain, anyway."

Alone in her father's garden, Kennedy took a fistful of the little stones from under her feet where they lay like an undulating carpet. She stood for a minute looking at the sky.

"Coming," she said quietly.

Shoving a few stones in her mouth, she rolled their smooth little bodies under her tongue and between her cheeks. They tasted like dirt but felt like candy. Her fingernails scraped the dirt as she knelt to gather more. The baby cried. She thought of Davey in the hospital with Fran and her mother, a sad and comforting triangle.

Bending down in the mist of a rain that would rupture the longest drought in Iowa, she emptied her lungs, let go of her breath, and filled her mouth with stones.

Practical
Anthropology

I.

"It's a living," Rita says. The other lap dancers take their
place on line behind her, arriving in clusters like ants to
a sugar spill. They create a distraction, making it hard for Rita
to catch Candy's eye. Although she is always first to arrive and
last to pay, Candy stands somewhere in the middle, inspect-
ing several pairs of stockings for visible rips while she waits to
pay her money. Shuffling through an oversize gym bag, she
lets out a quiet stream of expletives before looking up to meet
Rita's gaze.

"It might be, if they didn't rip us off so much."

Candy produces an empty diet Coke from her duffel
bag and tosses it at the cashier's window of the old theater,

which is protected by a bulletproof encasement, possibly for moments just like this.

Renaldo, engrossed in overcharging and misinforming, barely seems to notice Candy's assault. He waves, smiling at Candy and mouthing her name obscenely.

Daylight flashes every time someone else opens the metal door and lets it slam.

Renaldo licks his lips.

"My boyfriend's going to wrap his fingers around your skinny neck, asshole." Candy puts her hands on her hips.

The lobby smells of damp crotches and cigarette butts.

"But I might like that, Candy," Renaldo says into the microphone. His gravelly voice filters all the way through to the dance floors, echoing across the bald velvet chairs that in just a few hours will be filled with eager johns.

Right now the theater is empty; it's not quite 6 p.m. Most of the girls still need to settle some debts with Renaldo and score something. Some of them laugh at Candy, but most don't even notice. A few bracelets jangle; some heels click against the floor.

"Fuck you," Candy says softly. She smiles a little, pretending to take it lightly, to be a good sport, which she isn't.

Candy is Rita's favorite dancer. Unlike the others, she doesn't do a lot of smack or anything else, except a joint once in a while. Rita herself doesn't party very hard either—only when the urge hits. Usually she crashes with Candy, whom she knows from school, and Candy's college-professor boyfriend, Harold, who teaches English composition at Lang—not a bad guy, Rita thinks, though he occasionally gets out of control.

When Rita goes on drug binges and stays at Candy's place, she tells her girlfriend Mariveila that she is visiting her family, whom, in truth, Rita has not seen in several years; she doesn't know why it never occurs to Mariveila to call her mother and father to try to get an invitation. Maybe it's because she's a secretary, someone who knows how to sneak around reading other people's mail, overhearing conversations, uncovering real business. Or maybe it's because Mariveila is still so deeply in the closet. Whatever the reason, she never tries to verify Rita's story; Mariveila believes that Rita works for an architect named Renaldo Reyes on East 12th and has a job on campus in the dissertation room, shelving books and filing papers.

Candy's friends, and even Harold, know Rita only by her stage name; they call her "Maggie." Rita is impressed by the frequency with which Candy uses her real name. There are ancient messages in Mariveila's handwriting stuck to Rita's refrigerator that read, LOUISE CALLED.

"Who's Louise?" Mariveila once asked. "A professor?"

"Someone from Vassar," Rita answered. "She's thinking about getting a graduate degree in public health."

This is not a lie.

Occasionally Rita wonders what she would do if Mariveila ever found out how she really makes a living. On a good night, without tricking and after everyone's cut, she takes home about $600. Probably she'll never have to invent an explanation, though she's certain she could conjure up something plausible if it ever came to that. For now, the whole thing, Rita's life, seems perfectly believable.

Candy, a rare find, a bona fide straight stripper—as in *heterosexual,* as in *arrow*—is always having to defend herself from the other dancers, most of whom are either dykes or so strung out, they hang on to anything that moves, which Candy definitely knows how to do. Long-legged and a true redhead, Candy is stunning. Unlike most of the girls, she is as fresh as unchewed gum.

"C'mon, cunts," Renaldo says placidly into the mike from behind the solid encasement, "get off your asses and pay me my money."

Three dancers line up and give him the finger; Candy laughs so hard, she abandons her search for hosiery damage.

Rita laughs too, hoping vaguely to make a contribution.

The money Rita makes from stripping pays her tuition at the city university, where she is getting her Ph.D. in anthropology. The Melody, "an establishment for paying gentlemen," is a kind of fieldwork for Rita. In fact, her slightly removed attitude makes her popular among the customers, chiefly middle-aged business owners from Jersey and Connecticut, who ask for her by name.

No one ever gets the joke.

"Where's Margaret?" they yell through the smoky theater before taking their seats. "Where's Margaret Mead?"

All of the strippers have fake names, most of them more than one—custom-tailored personae that pump up the price of an after-hours trick and give the appearance that every john has his own personal girl. This illusion seems the least they can do. Rita tried on several aliases before finally arriving at this one two years ago while studying for her orals. The university had cut her scholarship, forcing her to turn tricks to stay enrolled.

Unlike the other lap dancers, Rita now employs a single identity, no matter what the circumstance, offering herself in one thin dimension like a dinner mint; it's all she can afford. No more wigs and costume changes—they get her the way she is: no makeup and the same old gray G-string with its spongy feel and stretchy elastic. When it gets hot, she pulls the straps off her shoulders and dances without a top. Also, since cutting off her hair just before her final semester of classes, she is nearly bald, but this latest fashion statement has turned out to be surprisingly lucrative.

"Do you know something?" Rita asks, periodically letting the customers in on an actual observation. "You remind me of my father." As if out of the blue, she'll say, "Do you want to know my last name?"

This seems innocent enough, and it always works. "Tell me, baby," the john always says.

It sometimes gets to her, the buttery way they talk, though she knows every last one of them is angling to get her out of the Melody, where the rules are strict.

In the main auditorium, the price of a partially sanctioned hand job is a third to the house. The transaction is fast: a quick wave to Renaldo to turn his back, unzipping the guy and roughly letting him have it, all the while saying the name over and over, mouthing it slowly like a jewel between her lips, believing at the moment that she truly is the Margaret Mead of lap dancing. The rush of activity is sometimes worth it, vaguely erotic, even to Rita. After it's over, she tucks the money into her G-string, where the elastic still holds, and goes to the next guy.

Everything about her job is classifiable, a fact Rita finds extremely satisfying.

II.

"Doing anything Sunday?" Candy asks.

They're in the basement locker room, which most of the dancers use as a closet or a hangout for getting high. Candy and Rita never come dressed, so usually they're left alone to struggle into their costumes. Sometimes Rita feels as if she is still in high school, getting ready for varsity soccer.

"Nope," she says, stepping into her G-string and adjusting it between her legs.

"Harold and I are driving down to Raleigh to see my old man. He's picking me up after work, and we're driving through the night. Romantic, huh? Anyway, the place is free if you need somewhere to crash. Just feed the cat."

"No, thanks," Rita says. "I visited the family last week; Mariveila might get suspicious."

"Suit yourself."

Usually Candy wears hot pants and a halter top, but today she is slipping into a shiny lamé bodysuit that fits like a glove and flares out just above the ankles. The neckline plunges like a steep cliff; cutouts decorate her thigh and back, exposing her beautiful white belly with a piece of missing fabric the shape of a flower. She bends over, slipping into a golden pair of matching platform sandals.

"New outfit?" Rita asks.

"Mmm-hmm, Harold picked it out. Like?" Using a broken shard of glass, which she leans against a hand dryer, she has to bend a little at the knee to see her reflection.

"Great," Rita says, reconsidering her own dress code. "My boyfriend was never that nice."

Candy shrieks. "*You* had boyfriends?" She holds a mascara wand out in the air, looking over at Rita.

"Boy*friend*," Rita corrects. "I almost married him."

A few stragglers getting high in a corner search around to see who's speaking.

Rita turns her back on them.

"Married?" Candy repeats, smiling. "So what happened?"

"He was in the Navy," Rita says.

"So?"

"So, by the time he screwed a few female officers and wanted me to be his Navy wife, I realized the world was a big place."

"Bigger than this?" a deep voice asks. Rita turns to see a disheveled dancer named Marsha standing against a bank of spray-painted lockers, indicating the whole room with an airy wave of her hand.

"You'd have been a Navy lesbian, anyway," says Andrea, a dancer Rita hates, hanging off the conversation, forcing an unreal trickle of laughter out of her mouth.

"Yeah, or…" One of the others, her drugs now peaking, tries to take her turn, but she's already started to fade.

Rita hates the way they make everything seem ugly. She likes the way they smell, though, when they're getting high—for that alone she doesn't mind their standing around making fun. It's as if each bead of their sweat had been rolled in baby powder and lemon peels and buried under dirt. The smell is so pungent, she doesn't know how the johns don't notice. Or maybe they do.

"Broke his heart, though," Rita says. "My mother still mourns the relationship. She hates all my girlfriends, says she wanted to be the only woman in my life."

"Sounds kinky," Candy says.

Rita has never thought about it, her mother being so religious and seemingly pure. Candy is probably right.

"Guys with broken hearts are always guilty," says June, everyone's dealer.

"Oh, c'mon, like she wasn't screwing everything in sight herself?" accuses one of the more coherent girls.

"I wasn't," Rita protests. "I was completely loyal. Even afterward. Well, except for the therapist."

No one speaks except Candy, who cuts her finger on the mirror shard, letting out a quiet gasp that sounds like a curse.

"Twice my age," Rita says, as if someone has encouraged her to continue. "Now *she* was a real mess." She gazes into her locker. "There ought to be laws against that shit."

"There are," Candy says flatly, running her bleeding finger under the faucet.

"Well, girl," June says, grabbing a rubber snake and frizzy yellow wig. "You had your virgin stage. Now welcome to your whore."

III.

Rita has always hated stripping. She watches from a dark corner as June twists herself into a back bend that appears to be an afterthought; the air seems charged during the first shift. Rita puts off her own strip until the end of the night, the third and final set; there's no escaping. Everyone watches the strip, and every girl is required to put on a show.

After June, when the lap dancing resumes, Rita feels herself relax.

The dread is usually worse than the actual work.

Finding one of her regulars, a sad-faced computer programmer barely surviving a nasty divorce, she lets the rhythmic music calm her. Each dance lasts two minutes; her usual rate is $10 per dance. There are rules: No customer can jerk off; no touching the dancers; pay at every pause. Sometimes the men get to press their palms against a crotch, moist or dry, depending on the dancer. The no-cum rule is difficult to enforce and rarely feels important, unless the guy is gross. Some guys can't seem to help themselves, but they are usually the meeker ones who get embarrassed easily. Rita doesn't care.

Her current customer, the computer programmer, peers at her dolefully.

"You'll live," she says, punching him on the shoulder. "It's only divorce."

"I bought my father a tie from Lord & Taylor," Candy says to Rita on their break. She presses a fresh layer of lipstick onto a Kleenex.

Rita grunts. "What's with the father fixation?" The subject irritates her.

"That's why we're here, isn't it?" interrupts Andrea. She has so many names, Rita can barely keep track: Cynthia, Gloria, Anastasia, Alice.

"Why are you talking to me?" Rita is feeling hotheaded—not a good sign. She gives a little shove to Andrea's shoulder. "Did you mistakenly think I was interested in your opinion?"

"Fathers, I mean, silly," Andrea continues, her eyes glassy, as if she's still lit up.

"Why are you always near me?" Rita says, feeling clearly disgusted. "Go away."

"Seriously," Andrea persists, pretending not to notice that both Rita and Candy have turned their backs. "Aren't we here because every day is Father's Day?"

Before Rita can get a good grip on Andrea, Renaldo shows up; she is turning on a heel when he catches her by the elbow. Renaldo always seems to sniff out a fistfight just seconds before it happens.

"Ladies, ladies," he says. "It's your time cards and your busted noses, but it doesn't make my customers happy to see you standing around bitching like their wives."

Everyone freezes, until Andrea manages to wiggle away, a weak little smile on her painted lips. Rita wishes she could kick Andrea for getting to her.

"Forget it," Candy says. "She says something stupid every night of the week."

"Fuck her," Rita says.

"Look, what does she know about your father or my father or her own father? She's a freak. Drop it."

Spotting one of her regulars, Candy disappears suddenly into the red-tinted darkness, leaving Rita to fend for herself.

Rita is glad to be distracted during her strip number, which is fairly unimaginative. She usually stands around, sneering and rocking a little to the music like a boy; to her surprise, everyone applauds and whistles, as if she were a master at the art of seduction. In her head, Rita tries to surrender to the lights, the stage, the beady eyes of customers and colleagues. Like being mugged, resisting the flow seems like a bad idea.

Rita hates it when people look at her.

When she was thirteen, Rita had a cousin who thought Jesus was molesting her, a girl who fell into trances at the drop of a hat. Rita's father, a dentist, was the only one in the family who'd been to medical school, so the girl's parents took her to see him, too embarrassed, Rita guessed, to find a real doctor, convincing themselves Rita's father was qualified to make a diagnosis by virtue of putting his hands in people's mouths. After a quick examination, he found that the girl suffered from petit mal seizures, a mild form of epilepsy. Not to worry, he said; she'd grow out of it.

Asshole, Rita thinks. Her eyes burn. The girl killed herself at age fifteen.

Standing in front of a seated older man, a regular in a seersucker suit, a low-level government official from Newark, Rita flicks her pelvis back and forth just above his thighs, butting his chest a couple of times. She finds a focus beyond his gaze and thinks about her dead cousin, Jesus, and her father, an unlikely trio. Before she knows it, she has her hand wrapped tightly around the guy's silk tie, yanking it taut.

"Hey, Margaret Mead," he says, excited at first. "Hey, get off me, bitch. Let go!"

With some satisfaction, she watches the guy's face flush. In seconds, it seems, Renaldo has her by the waist and is dragging her across the dance floor, through the hallway, and down the stairs to the locker room. She protests loudly, kicking as best she can, trying to hook her black army boots to the banister, but before she can get a good grip to resist, he tackles her. They roll down a few stairs to the bottom, where Rita is certain she hears a rib crack.

"You're out," Renaldo says, pressing harder on her with his lower body as he lifts his chest off her to get some volume. His knees stab her shins.

He jams a fist into the moldy carpet next to her face, inches from Rita's shorn head.

"I don't want to see your ugly face for the rest of the month," he says.

Panic flashes through her mind. Then her thoughts jump from Candy's keys to her dissertation topic: violence in sex establishments.

"I'm tired of this strangling shit, you whore." Renaldo is still on top of her, pushing his loose face in hers; his flesh hangs strangely. Rita looks at the ceiling. "Do you hear me?"

"Of course I hear you, asshole—you're screaming in my face," Rita says calmly through the chaos of her mind.

IV.

"Merry Christmas," the woman sitting on the milk crate tells Rita. Disdainful, she holds out an expectant hand, a white-looking palm held upward toward heaven. Rita stares at the large woman in a housecoat and torn men's leather slippers, wishing she'd just kept walking. The woman is positioned in the shade of a building, squeezed into a corner near the avenue just outside Candy's apartment, her ankles bruised like ripe fruit.

"Happy Halloween," she says, as if by some mistake Rita doesn't know the polite response is to fill her hand with coins. On this side of town, the trees grow out of the concrete like somebody's idea of a joke; the birds gather in packs large enough to hide a dead body.

The woman seems to smolder unpleasantly, a dark moon face surrounding white teeth.

Too hungover to dig for pennies, Rita pulls a pack of cigarettes out of her pocket, holding them out.

Shaking her head, the woman shifts and pulls back her feet. Her skin sticks out of the slippers like bread dough.

By the light stench now beginning to lift and dissolve in the heat, Rita assumes it is nearly 7 in the morning. Searching her bag for money, she tries to remember where she's been since her last coherent memory, her tangle with Renaldo at the Melody. The streets are beginning to warm, burning away another lousy Saturday night.

Rita wonders what she told Mariveila last night, where she scored, what she snorted, whom she fucked.

"You called your father?" the woman asks.

Like regurgitating unpleasant food, Rita experiences déjà vu. She remembers how she used to be her father's favorite, how he'd let her play in his den with all his rifles and the heads of animals he'd shot down. He'd helped her give them jungle names. Then, one day, when she was still a little girl, he simply stopped speaking to her, leaving Rita's mother to repeat her childhood stories like ghastly jokes: When she was three, Rita's father watched her run out into rush-hour traffic; when she was seven, he accidentally slammed her fingers in the car door; when she was twelve, he got her drunk on gin and tonic.

"What?"

"Father's Day," the woman persists.

Rita wishes Mariveila were with her. Mariveila doesn't believe in charity or strangers or striptease clubs; she believes in coming home early and graduate school. Mariveila would have grabbed Rita by the arm and maneuvered her around this woman; she would have found a safer passage, eyes above the pavement, head out of the clouds. She would have explained how Father's Day is nothing more than a way for Hallmark to make money. A capitalist plot, Rita would have told her girlfriend, who never seemed bored by her theories.

She'd probably left a message for Mariveila about a sick friend or an all-night study group in the library.

Now the air hurts Rita every time she breathes in.

"He's dead," Rita says, feeling revived by the thought of Mariveila.

"What about your husband, then?" the woman asks.

"Coronary heart failure," the words pulse evenly out of Rita's mouth. "Both dead."

The woman grunts, pulling her lips to the side, a gesture Rita doesn't know whether to read as sympathy or doubt.

"Shame," the woman finally says, eyeing Rita's closed hand.

Unable to locate a single coin, Rita has rolled paper money into her fist. She offers it absently: a one-dollar bill, evenly exchanged for a lie that for some reason makes her feel better.

V.

In the den of her childhood home in Massapequa—in the opposite direction of Rita's current path toward Mariveila, miles away from the squinting woman who held her momentarily in check like a giant black sun—Rita's father collects rifles and displays them in glass cages. He caresses the beautiful wooden edges, oils their muzzles until they shine. On the wagon for the third time this month, he tries to ignore the remnants of another sleepless night. He hasn't heard from his daughter in years. All he's got left is the nice clean aroma of gun oil.

"It's Rita," his wife, a woman forced by ordinary circumstances to surrender to appearances, whispers through the door.

Rita's father tries to remember.

"She's on the phone," his wife insists fretfully on the other side. She jiggles the doorknob, perhaps to jog his memory.

"Oh," he nods.

He tries to pinpoint the exact moment he first began to hate everything, but this seems impossible right now. At noon a dry gin martini will remind him.

He opens the door and lets her in.

"What?"

"It's Rita," she repeats. "She's calling for Father's Day."

He looks at her. From her excited face he concludes that Rita hasn't called home in a long time.

"Aren't you going to pick up?" she asks.

Long ago Rita's mother stopped wanting anything, knowing how easily what you want can be destroyed. Her own daughter illustrates the point—ruined, though she doesn't know exactly how. The time she found Rita in the basement with a broken ankle, not making a sound, the hammer still in her hand, poised above the crushed bone; she was only nine, ten at the most. A few years later, of course, there were nights when she never came home. *Ruined,* Rita's mother thinks, marveling at how fragile an innocent life can be. She watched the damage slowly creep in, as if through the bedroom window, and a film of depression hardened over her like a clay mask. She cannot even get angry now. Anyway, who would she be angry at? The Jesus she prays to every night, the Jesus who molested a fifteen-year-old girl, who allowed the ruin of her own daughter?

She stands in the doorway, waiting.

"Tell her I'm out," Rita's father finally answers.

"Please," Rita's mother says, but she feels exhausted, standing in the doorway waiting for something to happen, anything to happen.

By the time she remembers that Rita is on a pay phone and turns for the kitchen, shutting the door behind her, she is met by the flat buzz of a dial tone in her ear. Pressing the receiver back into its cradle, she listens instead to her onions burn in their pan, hissing in unison, as if at any moment they might call out her name.

Accommodations

The week before Rachel and I are to drive through the desert, my mother calls long-distance to say our baby sister is missing again. Relaying the news like an anchorwoman, she aims for a cool tone.

"I suppose that's all," she concludes after making her report. "The house is fine. How's the weather down there?"

"What hospital?" I want to know.

"I'm not sure." My mother sighs. Maybe the subject bores her. "She was in acting school, you know, New York City, off-Broadway, or off-off-Broadway, I forget which one."

"Right, but what happened?"

"No one knows," she says. "They think she walked out in a nurse's uniform."

My sister Ellie never loses her flair or ability to function. I can just imagine her convincing an entire staff of nurses that it's her turn to make the rounds, to dispense the meds. Then, calmly, before anyone notices, she slips down an elevator and out through the lobby, waving to the security guard, electric doors zipping her out into that city of strangers. It's hard to imagine sometimes that Ellie is as crazy as the doctors say.

One time, before my parents moved from Cleveland to California, I watched her pouring drinks at the local bar, striking up conversation, amusing the native Midwesterners with matchbook tricks, the whole time appearing unendingly sane. At the time, she'd checked out of the local psychiatric hospital, dropped out of high school again, and taken an apartment in the city near the outpatient clinic where my parents could still check on her. Home visiting, I had stopped on my way from the airport and stumbled across her charming the regulars. My parents hadn't known she'd taken a part-time job; they acted surprised but pleased.

"It's good for her to have a little distraction," my father had said.

I wasn't crazy about the bar: It seemed a little too distracting for my taste, and I never did ask Ellie about the wig.

"What was she in for this time?" I ask my mother, who is still on the line. "I thought she was doing better."

"I don't know. Someone at that acting school checked her in," my mother says. "I guess she'd been acting kind of strange—not literally, of course. Her acting was brilliant. It's her behavior they found odd."

"Did you call the police?" I say.

"Daddy's gone to look for her." She hesitates, then sighs: "New York's a big place, though."

"Yeah. And Daddy's a small man."

"Guess it won't be seder dinner without the birthday girl," my mother adds, beginning to sound resigned.

Last year we visited Ellie in New York for her birthday and had seder dinner at a restaurant in Chinatown, the whole family, my father gawking out the window at the crowded market streets, Ellie acting only slightly subdued, showing off with chopsticks. Fussing over Sammy, my mother suddenly proposed a traditional passover in California at their brand-new house, which none of us had yet seen. That was when Rachel offered to fly to New Mexico and drive up the coast with me and the baby. Ellie, who we've learned not to count on, said she didn't know if she could commit, but the more we talked about the desert and the seaside hotels we would stay in once we hit the coast, the more she liked the idea.

At the time it sounded like fun.

"Good thing you had Sammy, so someone can be our youngest," my mother says over the phone, affirming my deepest suspicion that in her mind all children are somehow interchangeable. "I wonder if I should cancel the cake?"

* * *

April is coming, and Ellie is afraid. All that talk about killing the firstborn makes her glad she is female, the last in line. A birthday party in California: bitter herbs, birthday cake.

Most people have been around forever, trying to fit the pieces together, to learn the lesson, to break their karma, to become some other form of life. It's not an easy thing to do. If she has the child she has just found out she's carrying, it might be more advanced than she is: a Leo, proud and unforgiving.

Just getting through this single life alone, she is overwhelmed.

* * *

During her last dramatic disappearance, Ellie had been studying abroad at a psychoanalytic institute in Sweden; that was four years ago—1984, to be exact—the year Ronald Reagan stayed in office another term, the year Ellie analyzed our dreams. The oldest by a decade, which embarrasses her somehow, Rachel offered to pay for Ellie's tuition, encouraging her to find a real profession, go to school, turn over a new leaf. A top executive at IBM, Rachel underwrites everything: Ellie's medical bills, her living expenses, fancy parties for our parents' anniversaries, family trips to New York and the lake.

"What are you trying to do, Rach?" my father always teases, "buy our love?" Rachel grimaces; she is a Republican, a lesbian who, like the rest of us, is unable to maintain a relationship, rendering the gender of love irrelevant. She doesn't like to talk about it. Still, Ellie and I have always envied Rachel, feeling that we were somehow young and empty, not very original, though Ellie does a better job at keeping up.

"The institute doesn't approve of disrupting people's sleep," Ellie told me three days before her 1984 disappearance from Scandinavia. "I can't figure out the time difference. What time is it there?"

I didn't mind her waking me: As her charts predicted, 1984 was also the year we were having nightmares.

"What's wrong, honey?" I said, slipping out of the bed where Sammy was quietly snoring.

"They don't like women here," Ellie whispered loudly into her end of the phone. Prior to the Sweden incident, she'd said the very same words from a phone booth at the University of Michigan, where she was trying her hand at art school. Two weeks after that, she'd simply slipped away.

The day Rachel and I are readying the car to drive up north to our parents' without Ellie, who still hasn't turned up, she arrives like a mirage with the sun, ambling toward the drive-way in torn jeans, as if she's been living out in the desert. Sammy is the one who spots her off in the distance.

"Look, Mommy," Sammy says, running circles around the car, its doors and hatch wide open like a black beetle stretching its hard outer shell. Arranging the backseat, Rachel looks up from the luggage before I have a chance to turn around, and I can see in her expression that Ellie has arrived just in time, her image shimmering in Rachel's sunglasses.

Despite her obviously fragile state, or maybe because of it, Ellie is radiant, a tangle of gold curls, a glow in her deep green eyes.

"I've got presents for you," she says to Sammy, who is running toward her. Like a magic trick, Ellie is pulling something soft and furry out of her bag, a terry-cloth rabbit.

It is too early to worry about traffic, but my heart strains to see the skinny backs of Sammy's five-year-old legs carrying her away from me.

"Where have you been?" Rachel says, annoyed.

We meet Ellie in the front yard, where the vegetation grows low to the ground, protection from the desert heat.

"Riding trains," Ellie answers.

"Are you okay?" I say, smoothing Sammy's hair and pulling her close.

"Look, Mommy." She holds up Ellie's gift.

"Pretty," I say, noticing how in Sammy's mind, Auntie Ellie has not been gone for more than a minute.

"I'm fine," Ellie says, giddy at the sight of her niece. "Oh, Sharon, look what you made!" she adds, lifting Sammy off the ground and holding her under the arms, as if at that very moment all the neighbors might rise at once from their beds, pull the shades, and look across the planned community of adobe-like houses to witness a miracle.

* * *

She wakes up every morning still surprised to find herself alive. Unplanned pregnancy is not the issue, though she wonders if it's bad luck to create a life out of violence.

The problem with the human race is not another baby: It's that people share only the good dreams, not the nightmares. Who ever talks about rape and hospitals and the mentally unstable? No one likes to bring it up.

It is in our nightmares that we are truly alone, Ellie thinks.

* * *

In dreams, Ellie told me once, houses represent our souls. At the time, she was sitting in my kitchen, her arms wrapped tightly around Sammy, who was then only a few months old, a tiny pink bundle she held against her beating heart. This was not long after my divorce. Ellie had resurfaced just in time to take up residence in the attic, offering me comfort and making miniature houses with tiny moving parts: closets that opened to reveal the linens, front-porch swings swaying in a minuscule breeze. She learned to make them at a workshop in New Hampshire, the location, it turned out, of her reappearance after dropping out of rabbinical school.

"They're like tiny broken promises," she said one day. "Dream houses."

After Sammy's father moved out, I hadn't wanted to let the baby out of my sight: I was certain she'd choke in her sleep or strangle to death in her sheets. Ellie thought it was a manifestation of my anxiety about being divorced; Sammy's dad thought I was insane. Whichever, I carted her around in a tote, even while she slept, and never left her alone.

This went on for months.

"What do hotel rooms mean?" I asked Ellie casually.

She stared at me long and hard.

"They're very, very bad," she said, a dark cloud passing over her expression.

"My dreams take place in hotel rooms," I said.

"So do mine," she whispered gravely.

* * *

Ellie is the first to admit the reason she's making replicas of houses: She is trying, little by little, to save her soul.

* * *

"Remember Charlie?" Ellie asks after we've been in the car awhile, driving toward the sprawling ranch our parents humbly call their retirement home. "What a good dog he was."

"Charlie was a terror," Rachel says.

"Who's Charlie?" Sammy says.

"My dog, my big, beautiful, fluffy dog," Ellie tells her.

"He had a few behavioral problems, I'll give you that," I say, "but he could sure fetch a ball."

I check the rearview mirror, which is angled so that I can keep an eye on Sammy, who is strapped safely in the seat next to Ellie.

"Remember how he destroyed the furniture?" Rachel says, laughing. "He was so stupid."

"Charlie was not stupid," Ellie says. I can hear the tide of her voice turning. "He was vindictive, a little scheming, maybe, but only when he didn't get his way. Never stupid."

"So how do you explain his eating six pounds of raw hot dog, then jumping into the lake?" Rachel says.

"He would have been fine if Uncle Manny hadn't egged him on," Ellie says.

"Uncle Manny?" I say.

"Uncle Manny didn't egg Charlie on, he tried to save him," Rachel says, turning partway around in her seat.

"Remember? We spotted Charlie thrashing around out past the big rock, and Manny jumped in after him."

"Yeah, I remember," Ellie says. "I remember that Manny never forgave Charlie for chewing up the inside of his convertible. I remember that he used to beat him with a garden hose. He was probably the one who fed him all those hot dogs in the first place."

In the rearview mirror I can see the heat rising in Ellie's face. Sammy, it appears, has lost interest and is dozing off, her small head nodding with the motion of the car.

"He did kind of take his time diving into the lake, Rachel," I say.

Rachel clucks her tongue and shoots me a look.

"Yeah," Ellie says. "First he took off his sunglasses, then he unlaced his sneakers, then he took off his socks, then he took off his watch, then he took off his shirt. Finally, after Charlie was nowhere to be seen, he dove in. Poor thing had sunk to the bottom like a stone."

"Charlie was a menace," Rachel says. "He tore up the furniture and ruined the interior of every car we owned."

"Oh, so he *deserved* to be murdered in the lake?" Ellie strains forward in her seat. "Of course, fitting punishment."

"Charlie was *not* murdered, Ellen," Rachel says. "It was an accident."

"Bullshit." Ellie sits forward all the way. I can smell her minty breath, her head appearing suddenly between mine and Rachel's. "Manny is a pig. Remember what he did to Sharon?"

At first Rachel doesn't answer. Out of the corner of my eye I can see them both in profile: Ellen, with her bronzed child-like face, and, inches away, Rachel, a darker, older, brooding version of the same expression. Rachel turns her face away but sighs loud enough for me to panic.

"What?" I say, lowering my voice so Sammy doesn't hear. "What did Manny do to me?"

Rachel mutters something I can't hear; she's facing out the passenger window.

"He grabbed your tit at seder dinner, that's what he did," Ellie whispers hoarsely, reveling in her victory. My breast proves some obscure point about a dog who has been dead for over thirteen years. "Real nice guy. Real animal lover."

"Uncle Manny? Mom's brother?" I say, wondering if we are talking about the same little Jewish man who owns a chain of delis in Cleveland and sends all his children to Harvard Law School.

"One and the same," Ellie says, almost chirping now.

Suddenly I wonder if we are talking about the same me.

"Uncle Manny. Reached right up in front of Elijah and everyone and copped himself a feel," Ellie says as if it were a nursery rhyme.

"No," I say weakly.

I glance at Rachel, trying to keep my eyes mostly on the flat desert road. I remember her once saying she was worried not only about Ellie's individual fate but also about the whole dubious generation of lost souls, Ellie's peers. Rachel claimed they needed saving. Now, looking at Rachel, who doesn't return my stare but nods her head resolutely, I wonder if she thinks we are the ones to provide restoration.

We drive in silence a few minutes, Sammy breathing heavily, deep into her nap. My stomach begins to sink lower than all the slopes of sand surrounding us on every side of the car.

"I can't believe this. Why don't I remember?" I ask.

"You were very upset," Ellie says. "It's hard to remember awful things like that."

"Did anyone *do* anything?" I ask, feeling trapped. "Did Mom say anything?"

"I don't think so," Ellie says.

She sits back in her seat, placing her shoulder closer to Sammy's head as if for her own comfort.

"Ellie started screaming at the top of her lungs," Rachel says flatly.

"Did I really?" Ellie says from the backseat.

"Typical family celebration," Rachel says, rolling her eyes in my direction.

"Well, good for me!" Ellie says, her mood suddenly defiant. "That was the right response. In fact, I'm going to start screaming, I'm going to organize a whole movement of screamers, a political campaign of resistance. Pretty soon women all across the country, from me to Nancy Reagan, will start screaming at the slightest provocation. Screams Across America, I'll call it. Female salvation from the mistreatment of pigs like Uncle Manny."

Ellie's voice is strong and high, verging on manic; it rouses Sammy, who makes a gurgling sound, then opens her eyes.

"Are we there?" she mutters.

"No, honey," Ellie says. "We're still here."

I glance to my right in time to see Rachel's dark curls swinging through the air. As she turns her head my way, I catch a glimpse of my mother, making me think that Rachel is already old, almost forty, and only a few years older than me. After Ellie has fallen asleep in the back with Sammy, finding our way safely out of the desert seems somehow easier.

"Let's get to the coast," Rachel mumbles. "I need some air."

* * *

It's nothing special. Ellie was born of a long line of lunacy that has nothing to do with her family of origin. Sometimes she watches for her real sisters, the ones who do not bear up, sometimes forgetting who she really is. It carries her right to the edge—

crossing against the light, driving too fast, making bad deci-
sions—because what's to fear?

It makes her think she should save a life and get herself an
abortion.

* * *

As soon as we are seated in the red plastic chairs of the
McDonald's at a California rest station, still twenty miles
from the ocean, Ellie launches breathlessly into one of her
exhausting stories.

"In the hospital two times ago—I think it was Michigan,"
she says, "there was this woman who tried to kill herself with
Drano, and she ended up in a coma, and after about a year
they found out she was five months pregnant."

Rachel and I glance at each other.

Sammy watches her as if it were a children's story.

"Well, it was pretty clear that one of those motherfucker
orderlies had knocked her up. Then come to find out, those
shitheads made it their regular business to rape helpless
patients at night when the nurses were making rounds. They'd
start at the opposite end of the floor, passing the nurses in the
middle, smiling just so, and no one was the wiser. Those poor,
poor girls."

She breathes heavily over her french fries, handing one to
Sammy, who greedily eats it up.

"Poor, poor girls," Sammy mimics.

For a minute my mind lands on Uncle Manny, as if the
two stories are somehow intertwined. For some reason, I'm
glad that my parents have moved away from Cleveland, a hot
spray of shame rushing through me. I'm suddenly afraid for
Sammy.

"Anyway, happy birthday to me," Ellie adds, concluding
her story. "How about the jungle house?"

She points Sammy's attention through the window to a tangle of metal bars and chain swings shaded by a plastic shingled roof, the whole thing brightly colored in green and red, yet somehow still depressing. A sign on the structure is decorated with monkeys. Nearby some teenagers are smoking cigarettes, standing in a loose arrangement resembling a protest march of some sort, though they are perfectly still. I have to remind myself what year it is.

"No, stay here," I say.

"You can watch us through the big picture window," Ellie says, already taking Sammy's fragile hand and leading her past our table.

"Be careful," I say. "Watch her."

"It's okay," she says, out of hearing range; I read her lips, not wanting to let either of them out of my sight.

It is all I can do to stay in my seat. Rachel seems lost in her thoughts.

"What now?" she says as soon as Ellie reappears on the other side of the glass window, smiling and waving as she hoists Sammy up on her shoulders.

As if watching TV, I try to capture the story unfolding before me: Ellie, a twenty-four-year-old girl, carrying Sammy, a skinny five-year-old, my daughter, on her shoulders. Light-years above them, the sun is burning in a bright arc across the endless desert, pulling them out of focus, creating the illusion that they are not really the point.

"You ever dream about hotels?" I ask Rachel suddenly, but she doesn't answer, too busy providing her own interpretation of the child carrying the child past the circle of children as they reach the shaded distance and almost disappear.

Lucy on the West Coast

"Haven't you ever felt like someone was missing from your life?" Lucy Fernandez asked her mother. "Like you've lost someone important?"

It was San Francisco, 1995: People were always on the verge of dying or getting lost.

"I lost my keys once," her mother answered. They were sitting on a second-hand sofa in Lucy's apartment.

"That's not what I mean," Lucy said.

Her mother, still sweaty from working all day in a non-air-conditioned taxi, was drinking a glass of water. "I never know what you mean, *Mijita*. Have you been taking your medicine?"

Lucy rolled her eyes. The subject of illness was beginning to wear on her, especially when it gave her mother the opportunity to criticize.

When Lucy first disclosed her news, her mother had cried, hooking a brown arm around Lucy's neck and hanging there like an overcoat. Lucy, who just moments before had felt important, suddenly felt distant and queasy, as if her mother were putting on a show. Once she pulled away, dried her face, and begged Lucy not to talk about AIDS in front of her brothers, Lucy felt more normal. She hadn't wanted to tell them anyway. For the most part, Lucy and her three siblings orbited their mother like cold moons in separate spheres, barely coexisting.

Now Lucy's mother examined her, searching for clues. "Are you pregnant?" she said at last.

Panic rose and beat its wings against Lucy's ribs. Often she left her mother sitting in the hospital parking lot and went directly to the maternity ward to stand before a big picture window and watch the newborns in their Plexiglas cages. Had her mother somehow discovered that instead of visiting her doctor, Lucy had been spending those hours smiling at nurses, watching babies wail and squirm, engaging in casual conversation with new fathers and overly enthusiastic grandmothers? It was easy to supply her own details, pointing out a baby's tiny mole, telling a story of the hardships of premature labor as if she'd been through the experience herself. Lucy wasn't entirely sure why she did this—perhaps for the sympathy of strangers.

She looked at her mother's sweaty face. "Of course I'm not pregnant."

I'm a twin, she almost said.

Lucy was at work when she first read the story about the identical baby boys separated at birth, written up by some famous researcher who wanted to know if human loss could be measured. Lucy couldn't understand why they wasted time studying something whose answer was so obvious. The twins' lives had remarkable similarities, as it turned out: Both men were named Jim by their adoptive parents, and both had married small blond women named Elizabeth (one went by Bissy, the other, Lizzy). Both fathered three offspring—all girls, no twins—with similar names, and each Jim also had a dog he liked to take for a run around the block: two royal standard poodles named Buffy.

"Weird," Iris remarked, leafing through the glossy pages of a magazine.

"What's it prove, though?" Lucy asked. She was pulling a Tupperware container of yellow rice and beans out of her bag.

"Good question," Iris said.

It was lunch. The other social workers and administrative assistants were buzzing around like a swarm of hornets, warm with gossip and take-out burritos. Most of the staff already knew about Lucy; she'd taken each of them aside separately to impart the select details of her tragedy, until there was no one left to inform. At first everyone seemed impressed and rather nervous, but soon enough they went back to normal, as if collectively agreeing to forget, as if they'd never heard of HIV.

Though Lucy didn't believe researchers had the right to meddle in the perfectly good, well-matched lives of innocent people, one detail in particular about the twins stayed with her. When the Jims were finally informed about one another, nearly thirty years later, each remarked that he had always felt keenly that something was missing. "They probably said it at the exact same moment," Iris said, lifting an eyebrow in Lucy's direction.

Lucy clucked her tongue.

"Fucked up, messing with people's lives like that," Iris added.

Lucy pictured what it must have been like for the twins just moments before they learned the hidden truth, separated by a soundproof room, wondering what it was all about. She felt exactly the same way, she decided: She was on the verge of discovering whatever it was she'd irrevocably lost in the course of living. Her life, after all, was riddled with puzzles too: a father who'd walked out on her twenty years before, leaving no explanation. Not to mention her skin.

Lucy's mother was brown and creamy, like a tall glass of refrigerated chocolate milk. Her brothers were also dark, like matching pieces of well-done toast with fine, dark edges. Even the pictures of her long-departed father made him seem swarthy and tan, as if the island's sun had singled him out.

"It is strange, *Mijita*," Lucy's mother always said. "Maybe even lucky."

But Lucy didn't see it that way at all. She felt watery and insubstantial. *I live inside an off-white body with washed-out skin and nothing to keep me safe,* she often thought, imagining all the harmful matter in the world that longed to invade the hard-to-see borders of her flesh. She rubbed her freckled eggshell arms.

If I'm not careful, she told herself, *I'll really come down with something.*

Lucy Fernandez worked at a large day-care facility for the mentally retarded, whom she was supposed to refer to as "the challenged." She had few qualifications for the job besides a sympathetic face, a bachelor's degree from a technical institute in New York, and a manner that could be described as no-nonsense. Her supervisors felt these qualities sufficed.

Six years ago Lucy and her mother had moved to California to join Lucy's brothers in the corporate moving company they had founded and then promptly run into bankruptcy.

For no reason she could think of, aside from a need to pay rent, Lucy had applied to be the assistant to the clinical director of the San Francisco Association for the Mentally Retarded. Her mother, meanwhile, took a temporary job driving a taxi, only to discover that she liked striking up conversations with unfailingly polite strangers who'd lost their way around the city by the bay.

Lucy liked being on the other edge of the continent, though she had continued her bad-luck streak of choosing inappropriate companions, gay men with very little time left, who were far too interested in convincing her that she was a lesbian or a fag hag. In truth, Lucy didn't like women very much, except for Iris; she was afraid of them. She also feared any man who might seriously consider taking her for a lover, which was probably why all her past boyfriends had turned up either gay or dead.

By the time she had moved out west, Lucy had given up on love altogether. She was vaguely content to be the kind of simple, pretty, clear-complexioned woman gay men find palatable, even useful. Sometimes they made her feel less lonely, though she really became part of their social lives only when they got sick and needed her. With most of the gay men she met, Lucy shared the vague quality of never quite being able to justify her life.

She found herself returning to the idea of the twins study, identifying profoundly with the Jims. It struck her at odd moments that she too had been separated at birth.

Lucy had to press down hard in her daily planner to scratch out the names of the missing and the dead; otherwise, it seemed like nothing more than lunch being canceled. Along with everyone else, though, she learned to ignore the paradoxes and unsolved mysteries, to put to rest each new disappointment, and, as much as possible, to enjoy the scenic view. The apartment houses on her sloping drive were all very cheerful, like flawless rows of pastel chalk, despite the fact that the air was damp and salty, as if perpetually filled with sorrow, especially when the weather was cool.

Of course, not all of the ghosts had died of AIDS. Don, for instance, was HIV-negative, but overdosed after a lifetime membership in NA and a career move back to New York City.

"They found him behind his desk on the stock exchange floor," a nervous midnight caller said into Lucy's phone. "They shut down the board for twenty minutes."

Lucy tried to imagine white men in ties and pressed shirts, shouting about dollars and yen over her dead friend's body.

"I'm just going through his Rolodex," the stranger apologized, long-distance; he realized that he had awakened her from a sound sleep.

Lucy had just been out to visit Don the month before; they had held hands while walking around the Village trying on leather jackets. He must have been consciously trying to fool her, Lucy surmised; she had no idea until they emptied out Don's apartment and found the bloody socks that he was shooting up between his toes.

"Once a junkie…" Richard had said.

In truth, there were very few people whom Lucy had ever loved, despite her mother's usual protest: "*Mijita*, why do you waste your time on *maricónes*?" Even so, her mother seemed fond of Lucy's friends. When Baker's landlord had rented the apartment out from under him the day of his boyfriend's funeral, Lucy's mother had taken him in until he died on her living room sofa, which folded out into an extra bed.

Lucy loved Don, of course, and Richard, who had gotten drunk once in college and made a pass at her; this was months before Richard and Don broke up. It was late; she hadn't had the energy to protest, and he was apparently having an important identity crisis. In the morning they went for breakfast at the campus cafeteria as if nothing special had happened.

Richard never got tested, but given that he'd been with nearly everyone in the Bay Area and, before that, in four of New York's five boroughs, what were the odds?

About three weeks after Lucy had marked his passing in her appointment book, she spotted him driving on Van Ness in an economy-size rental car, as if he'd never run that red light and killed himself. The dead could appear in the bodies of the living and make their presence known, Lucy realized. She had tailed him nearly to Fisherman's Wharf, before making a sharp U-turn, praying for no cops. After Richard left the body of the ordinary black guy, who tooted his horn and waved, Lucy began taking her special ability to mingle with the dead seriously.

She made notes in her calendar on the days she'd seen ghosts: Dave in the popcorn line at the movies, November 16th; Craig in Chinatown at her oldest brother's favorite restaurant on her mother's birthday; and Justin in the ladies' room at the Nikko Hotel on Secretaries Day, occupying the body of some guy who'd wandered in by accident, surprising a group of conferees checking their makeup. Lucy had let out a peal of laughter and rushed past the attendant, trying to catch him before he got away.

She could never predict when the sightings would happen or exactly who might appear around what upcoming corner, but she noticed that the ghosts had a dizzying effect on her. They wore her out, slipping through cracks in the universe and delivering strangely wearisome messages: "Hi" and "Excuse me." She imagined them as thieves—Craig, Dave, Richard, Don, Baker, and Justin—in it for the thrill, a kind of private joke that only she found funny.

Richard, her first ghost, vaguely resembled her father, according to the pictures her mother cut out and kept in tiny magnets on the dashboard of her car, as if at any street corner Lucy's father might hail her down. The whole front seat of her mother's cab was filled with cracked family photographs, snapped either in Puerto Rico or from far off a porch in Brooklyn. They featured a youngish dark-skinned man with close-cropped hair and flashing eyes, the man who had disappeared between the time Lucy was nine and eleven, taking with him her entire memory of the past. Whenever Lucy tried to recall those years, a black hole stared back at her. For a while, until the car accident, Richard filled up the emptiness with jokes and his vague resemblance, but most recently she saw something else emerge, something pleasing—the gleaming answer to her terrible ache: identical twins.

Lucy Fernandez wore her hair in tiny braids, dozens of braids, which hung to the shoulder on both sides of her perfectly shaped head. She wore a tiny silver moonstone on the end of each neatly arranged row, so that when she walked, it sounded like rain. It had been either her hair or her firm, upturned breasts and tight 501 jeans that first attracted her new boss.

"I heard he once screwed David Geffen," Jésus, the receptionist at the Association for the Mentally Retarded, told Lucy one day.

"No, Papi, not David Geffen," said Jésus's supervisor, Rafael, who happened to be standing at the fax machine listening in on the conversation. "David Geffen's boyfriend."

"Who's that?" Jésus wanted to know, swiveling in his chair.

"Beats me."

"Lame," Lucy said, delivering her editorial pronouncement on the quality of the information.

"Not lame, Mami," Jésus protested. "Just a little hazy."

"Let me know when you get something real," Lucy said, returning to her own desk.

Before Lucy's boss became the clinical director at AMR-San Francisco, he sold buildings for a living, acquiring considerable sums of money on questionable deals. Van Silver still dabbled in real estate as a sideline. At every office party and picnic, he invariably surrounded himself with slender Latin guys, whom everyone in the agency knew he liked to screw. At conferences he had them coming and going at regular intervals. Lucy knew from his messages, which she neatly transcribed from the office machine, that Van Silver both dated and swindled whomever he pleased, though she hadn't noticed any women in the mix.

"Why do you hang around all those gay men?" he demanded abruptly one day as she was handing him a mug emblazoned with the AMR-SF logo and filled to the rim with coffee. He drank it black.

"I thought you was gay yourself," Lucy said defensively. "I mean, *were* gay."

"I am," he said.

A wide, dirty smile crept across his uneven face, which was too big for his lumpy body and pencil-thin neck. "But I always wanted to have some pretty Latin babies. Interested?"

He winked at her.

At first Lucy couldn't speak.

"You're kidding, right?" she said. She tried to laugh, just in case he was.

"No." He looked her over impassively. "You like men, don't you, Lucy?"

"No," she answered automatically. "I don't."

"Don't tell me you like women?"

"Here's your messages," she said, slapping a pink handful on his desk.

He reached across a stack of papers to grab her hand, but Lucy slipped from his grasp. Her sterling bracelets made a slightly musical sound as she fled into the hallway.

He followed.

"Come on, Lucy, don't be like that."

All of Lucy's gay friends seemed to admire Van Silver from afar. Jésus said he looked like a plumber, from which Lucy surmised that all gay men must want to be screwed by ugly, balding, ill-mannered straight-looking men in rumpled, greasy clothes. In staff meetings he was constantly adjusting his penis.

"Not in one million years are you getting anywhere near me," she said loudly, shrinking at his breath on her neck and catching him off-guard as he tried to inch nearer, smelling of vegetable stir-fry. "I'd rather do anyone in this whole agency—male or female—than let any part of you touch any part of me."

She jabbed her painted fingernail directly into his wrinkled brown golf tie, which was festooned with little yellow men bent over five-irons.

"Watch it," Van Silver said, blinking furiously and taking a step backward. "A girl could get fired for a comment like that."

"Fuck you," she said, facing off squarely in front of her computer.

"Excuse me?" Van Silver's face turned red, as if he'd just been slapped.

"I said, I quit." Lucy curled the corner of her lips into the tense approximation of a smile.

"What? Again?" she heard someone say. In the conference room doorway, a crowd had apparently gathered.

Lucy picked up her handbag, pulled her toothbrush out from the top drawer of her desk, and walked to the elevator without turning back around.

"You can't quit," Van Silver shouted.

When the elevator finally opened its doors to let her inside, Lucy heard Van Silver mutter the word "bitch."

Stopping on her way home to buy a Frosty at the drive-through, Lucy cheered herself up with the idea of her long-lost twin, who lived somewhere on the East Coast and had also probably quit her job that day. Her East Coast twin (also named Lucy) marched into somebody's office and threatened a nasty lawsuit. But on the West Coast, the people at AMR-SF were so much like Lucy's family, she knew she'd never sue; she also knew, for better or for worse, that there was no escaping them. Luckily, before she had time to dwell on this depressing thought, she was distracted while backing out of Wendy's by a glimpse of Don, peddling down the sidewalk on a red ten-speed Raleigh. Lucy reacted quickly: Slamming on the breaks, she threw her mother's car in reverse, ignoring the horns from the traffic behind her. She refused to budge, until the car in her rearview mirror conceded to back up the hill to the place where Don was coasting without any hands. She rolled down the window and yelled to him.

"Hey," she said, feeling a rush of adrenaline.

"Hi," Don said.

Despite the early hour, a five o'clock shadow was beginning to overtake his handsome face. Before any other words could be exchanged, Don evaporated like a mist from the body of a young, skinny paperboy. On his own again, the boy looked confused; he whizzed out of control, as if he might crash into a mailbox.

"Watch out," Lucy yelled, shifting her mother's car back into drive.

She supposed it could have been her longing for the dearly departed that made them appear so haphazardly out of nowhere, commandeering some passerby's body and creating a public scene. Soon, though, she realized that she wasn't really longing for them; she was merely longing, and they were a convenient vehicle in which to carry out this elusive emotion.

Back at home Lucy hung her mother's keys on the hook by the door, playing her messages. Her mother had called, no doubt having heard the story from Iris.

"You think you're the only one in the world who ever had a boss say something disgusting?" her mother's voice echoed on Lucy's machine. Before she even had time to react, her mother said, "By the way, *Mijita*, I tried to call your doctor today. The hospital didn't have a listing for him. I must have the wrong name."

Lucy sat on her wooden floor, the wings of panic beating, then crawled into bed, where she stayed until noon the next day. Her mother called several times during the evening, her voice increasingly hysterical.

No one else called except Iris. Of course, almost everyone she knew was dead.

By two, when Jésus called with an offer to bring by some lunch, Lucy had developed a nervous fever; this perhaps explained the visions appearing behind her eyelids in crisp and colorful detail whenever she tried to nap. Over and over Richard bumped up against the car's ceiling like a rag doll with a soft, flimsy neck. It felt as if it were happening to her.

"You look like hell," Jésus said when he arrived with a plastic container of soup and a six-pack of diet Coke.

"I'm sick," she said.

"Van said if you apologize, you can have your job back."

He handed her the soup and chose the only piece of furniture suitable for his tight black jeans, a tan La-Z-Boy recliner. He lit a cigarette.

"*Por favor*," Lucy said, "I'll go back on Monday and do as I please."

She started to cough.

"You really are sick," Jésus said, sounding alarmed. "You wanna go see your doctor? What's his name?"

Lucy shook her head. She was afraid of doctors; this made her situation precarious.

"Braverman," she said automatically, sleep closing in fast. "Grossman, I mean." The next time she opened her eyes, Jésus was gone, and her room was dark.

The phone rang, startling her. Her mother's angry voice came over her machine as she stumbled to the bathroom.

"Lucia, I'm not kidding. Pick up the phone. I talked to Jésus. He says you're really sick. I need to talk to you, *Mijita*, about these doctors' appointments. Have you been skipping them? I'll kill you if you have. I'll kill you before anything else gets the chance."

Lucy's mother paused, waiting for her to pick up the phone. Lucy stood perfectly still in her sweatpants and T-shirt in the middle of the apartment. It was only a matter of time.

As she went back to her room, the closet behind the bed seemed to bulge out of proportion. She stared at it, rubbing her eyes. The light was on in the closet; she didn't think she'd left it on. The answering machine flashed an angry red eye at her. Lucy felt itchy all up and down her legs. She quickly opened the closet door.

"Jésus?" she said.

Pulling her bathrobe aside, she saw that it was Lew, who had died of sepsis on an airplane about three years earlier. She was the one who had gone to the airport to identify the body.

"Hi," he said.

"You're dead," she said.

"Technicality."

"I'm crazy?" she asked.

"Indeed," he said.

It took almost every ounce of energy Lucy had to move the heavy oak desk to the hallway. Lew stood around unhelpfully the whole time, his eyes as big as blue glass plates, expressionlessly watching her work.

"Why am I not surprised?" she asked, pushing past him to unplug the phone. Now no one would be able to open the door, maybe a crack or two at most. She considered sealing the windows, but that felt like too much work. When she finally lay back down and closed her eyes, she could smell Lew's rancid, peppery flesh, just as it had smelled in first class the day of his death. Even the flight attendants had evacuated while Lucy stood beside his stiff, pale body, answering questions from police officers suspicious of foul play.

"You're shivering," Lew said, piling a couple of blankets on top of her.

She was afraid to open her eyes and look at him; he had seemed kind of stringy beside her shoe rack. She tried to breathe through her mouth.

"Sorry about the stench," he said.

"It's okay."

He slipped under the covers.

"Do you mind if we nap?" she asked. "I'm so tired."

"You go ahead. I'm going to watch TV."

There was a movie on with Rod Steiger and Lee Remick called *No Way to Treat a Lady*. Lee Remick was a pretty good actress, Lucy decided, and pretty. She was drifting off into a vision of a beautiful blond woman nursing her back to health when she heard them standing outside her apartment door.

East Coast Lucy lived in Prospect Heights, the side of Flatbush Avenue where white people didn't usually go. Unlike her West

Coast twin, about whose existence she was blissfully ignorant, she slept with whomever she wanted—primarily glamorous lesbians, but sometimes smooth-faced hustler boys who resembled beautiful women when their blond heads hit Lucy's pillow.

"Just because you're a dyke," her friends warned, "you're not immune."

East Coast Lucy found out her status by accident while donating blood in 1988. As it turned out, she had 400 T cells—not a bad count, but not good either. A volunteer and eventual client at The Gay Male HIV Clinic on 34th Street in Manhattan, she became a poster girl of sorts, justifying the money the clinic received to treat women with AIDS, although there never seemed to be very many other women at the facility. At her regular doctor's appointments, the waiting rooms were teeming with young women of all kinds desperate for help. Lucy tried to put it aside, speaking at talkathons, dancing at "Parties for Strength," and generally doing whatever they asked. She liked the attention.

West Coast Lucy knew her twin, or hundreds like her, existed somewhere in Brooklyn. The thought was strangely alive and hopeful, providing her the perfect explanation for everything in her life that had recently gone wrong.

"Don't tell me you know what you're talking about!" Lucy heard her mother's hysterical voice outside her apartment door. There seemed to be a crowd banging on something, jimmying the knob as if the building were on fire. Lucy wondered if her makeshift blockade would hold them off. It was all she ever wanted—to keep people from getting close and finding out too many of her secrets.

The sound of Iris's cough surprised her; maybe the jig really was up. Iris was saying something in an attempt to interrupt Lucy's mother, but to no avail.

"*Shut up!*" her mother said when Jésus shyly tried to intercede. "*At least my friends know whether or not they have AIDS.*"

To get a better earful, Lucy peeled the sheet back, but now there was only silence, even from Iris, who was most likely the one trying to push the door open. The walls of Lucy's apartment shook with each effort.

Then she heard a male voice.

"She's your daughter, for Christ's sake," it said. "Why are you taking it out on them?"

Lucy had to think hard to place the voice. It was low and irritated. Its owner was trying a new strategy, it seemed, attempting to pry open the door with something metal. The voice belonged to her oldest brother.

"*I'm the one!*" her mother screamed. "*Who do you think has been taking her to the doctor for the past two years?*"

Lucy heard a door slam and then her neighbors' low voices. She thought of all the hours she'd stood in front of the newborn babies or wandered the cafeteria, looking for someone to talk to. She was definitely afraid of doctors.

"*Don't tell me she's my daughter! She made it all up. There isn't any Braverman or Grossman!*"

More silence.

"*Let me tell you something,*" her mother continued yelling. Lucy wondered if her voice would ever give out. "*She doesn't even have AIDS!*"

"My sister has AIDS," Lucy said calmly to Lew, who eyed her knowingly. Then as explanation, she added, "We're twins. You can understand the confusion."

"Of course," he said.

The sound of the door cracking open startled Lucy. She sat up abruptly. As soon as he realized that the desk in front of the door wouldn't push back far enough to let even skinny Jésus slip inside, her brother swore. Soon, Lucy knew, someone would think of taking the door off its hinges. She wondered if her twin's family (adopted family) was as smart. In the background she could hear Jésus saying this was cruel. He didn't believe it was a hoax. He sounded like he might cry, though. Iris was as silent as a stone. Lucy could imagine her fleshy face set like cement, her eyes hard. That was the problem with women: They turned on you eventually.

Even in the beginning, Lucy had known that eventually someone would find out. Van Silver would be impressed, though; she would see it in his eyes on Monday morning. At least, he'd be too afraid to mess with her again.

"*Mijita!*" her mother screamed through the opening. Her voice echoed impressively throughout the apartment. "*How could you do this to me?*"

Lucy looked at the ceiling. She was alone again. It was just like Lew to leave her in the lurch; he wasn't one for scenes. But it didn't matter; she'd traveled so far now, she had surpassed even her own fears.

For a moment she wished her brother wasn't standing out in the hallway with a screwdriver, methodically working his way inside, but as she fixed her eyes on the ghosts dancing in pairs against the dark gray background of her apartment like dozens of twin phantoms, she wasn't afraid at all.

Old Country

Assunta came from the Old Country, but north. "Northern Italy," she used to say, though it was barely so, a fingernail at most, a mapmaker's squint. I looked it up in an Army-issue atlas after my husband died. They sent me a registered letter and a box of his belongings: keys, some photographs, an atlas. Nothing about those possessions seemed familiar, not even the pictures. When they didn't send his body, I worried it was a mistake.

In Reggio we knew Assunta's people: Peasants who lived up the road, one village closer to the sea, they'd left for America before leaving was predictable. That was the only difference between her people and mine: a couple of miles, a couple of years. In the Old Country everyone's family worked in the orchards, shamed by the soil and the sickly trees that swallowed up olives before we could pick them.

What was the point in putting on airs?

Perhaps to an American eye, we seemed close, but in truth Assunta and I regarded each other with dislike. "Never let another woman into your heart," my mother always said. "It is ruinous."

We walked together to markets, speaking of daily concerns, a habit that helped us keep track of the living while reminding us of the dead.

Every morning we met for coffee, but it should be stated outright that I was never one to call her *compara*. I never forget another's sins, nor could I ever bring myself to overlook her betrayal.

"A tradition is a tradition," my mother used to say, and there was something compelling in that. Assunta's face reflected the white sun and dry air, the steel mountains of my mother's country. Just by standing there, tall and dark-eyed, she made me remember what I'd left behind.

Though many years have come and gone, I still remember what passed between us. It happened like a change in the weather: One day she simply passed under my window without stopping to get me, a rainstorm, a cloud, sneaking by. Not so much as a word. For almost seven years she did not stop. My husband was long dead even then, my children halfway grown; Assunta evaporated from my day, as if women no longer needed to wash and sinners no longer needed the sacraments.

Of course, there wasn't a servant at God's Sacred Heart who didn't watch her take up with the DeCastanza girls, widows from the war, two streets west on Culver Boulevard. They were Abruzzi and had married Mafia, or at least there were rumors.

At first, mistrusting my own eyes, I lived from morning to morning, watching behind curtains, looking through the glass, peering out the side door. I was used to observing her life, but never from the outside. Every one of us from the Old Country watched behind curtains, expecting to find our own reflection, a fragment of something we'd carried on our backs from Italy. "*Compaesano,*" the old men used to say. You used to be able to count on the familiarity. But during those days, even Assunta seemed like a stranger. Finally the silence became familiar, and eventually, as always happens, absence turned to relief. To ward off her curse, I said the *malòcchio* every night. I never witnessed a single evil spirit crossing my back fence.

Dominic the butcher was the one who told me that Assunta referred to me in public as *regina,* as if I were the one denying my heritage, making up stories about my blood. This insult the butcher overheard himself—or possibly his wife picked it up in the church parking lot where they gathered after mass, gum-chewing Abruzzi girls, fat as cows.

No one had much money in those days, but Assunta and her friends never seemed to be lacking.

"No one is prouder than a *Calabrese* woman," my father used to say, and standing at the butcher's counter, I knew he was right. I absorbed Assunta's insult as if learning of another's bad fortune. I nodded, even smiled, collecting several packages of meat, free from the wartime restrictions, from ration tickets and everything demeaning.

"Nice day," I answered.

I could feel Dominic's eye follow me through the store and out onto the street, just as my father might have watched over my departure.

Soon everyone knew what had happened. It wore on me well, like a smart new dress, the kind in those days I could never have afforded.

Then, one morning, as if nothing had passed—no years, no sorrow, no Sundays at Mass—Assunta returned to my back door with fresh cannoli. I poured her coffee in the usual cup. We sat discussing our gardens, as if we had never silently knelt side by side in the hot sun without a word, ignoring each other while scrupulously keeping track. There was no mention of the DeCastanza girls or insults. We sat and listened to a fan whir from the other room. I had more important things to think about: my daughter getting married, my son going off to a brand-new war.

After my children were gone, everything started to shrink— the neighborhood I knew, the places I could walk—even my heart became wrinkled and dry, an olive from a peasant's orchard. The neighborhood grew noisy and dangerous; even Dominic closed up his shop. There were rumors about his son; people refused to buy the meat. I stopped answering the door when the young man came around to shovel the snow or mow the lawn. I breathed in the air, no longer able to detect the scent of frying dough or garlic hung on the doorpost, only garbage and a hint of yesterday's coffee. And when the young black man came to the house to rake the leaves, I slipped ten dollars under the door and yelled instructions through the glass.

Sometimes, even now, angels stand on my bedstead to speak of Assunta, though I've forgotten their names.

"What penance did she offer?" they ask me.

After those seven years, she came every morning without fail. We walked to the grocery, to church to arrange Masses for my dead children. We armed ourselves against strangers and prayed at my husband's empty grave. All along she accompanied me, with never an errand of her own or complaint. In truth, she was patient as a nun.

I must never forget the day Assunta came back to my door and kissed me on the lips, like a man. The angels will not let me rest until I remember that Judas' kiss, though I, for one, have always admired that Judas said out loud what everyone else was thinking. Jesus was not free of treachery; he talked in rhymes, tricking and testing the others, his friends. Besides, no one is ever totally innocent, not even God.

I, myself, looked the other way, just as Jesus might have, though there she stood, a foot taller, a half-size thinner, in her lace-up shoes costing more than my meals for a week, her hair pulled away from her face, as if to remind me of a life I'd once led. A healthy figure, young and rosy, in the doorway of my husband's home, she stood there with her dark eyes blank, as if she had just earned a sack of coins.

I took a breath, drawing myself straight-shouldered backward, biting the inside of my cheek. This was not a true response but the act of committing to memory what I would someday have to use against her for all those days in silence.

I took the pastry from her hands and went to the stove, where I had set the coffee to boil. I hadn't heard the door, so I thought she might have gone in shame. Instead, she quietly slid into a chair at the kitchen table and waited for me to say something.

I spoke for a good twenty minutes about my departed husband, about my children, whose lives were linked with tragedy. I filled her in on all the daily events she had missed, until at last I said something she wanted to hear.

"Is that what you learned from the DeCastanza girls?" I asked, my eyes burning. She understood that I meant her kiss.

She stared out the window, watching sadly, as if at that very instant all our remaining days were turning to seasons.

"I never learned that from anyone." She said it carefully, as if the words had to be knotted at the end lest they fall apart completely.

She had never married nor even had a suitor; she had lived in that old house with her parents and, after they died, with her brother. He was a good man, although jealous of everyone. He didn't like how close I was with his sister; he was jealous of my husband as well. You could see it in his face. But he was good to her until his very last day.

Even after he'd fallen off that ladder, you could sometimes pull aside the curtain and see them, brother and sister, bent over a radio, listening for news or the weather, as if no one had died.

Just before what would have been my fiftieth wedding anniversary, Assunta disappeared again. My children had stopped coming, even before they died, the angels bringing me their news. I tried to count back on the church calendar to figure the days, but from the pencil markings it seemed that three weeks had passed without Assunta's visit. By then her hair was fully silver, but her eyes were flat and gentle, as if she were still young.

I smelled the musty rooms of my house.

The Virgin Mary looked down at me from the top page of the calendar with great kindness as I counted back again.

Three Sundays.

I pulled on a scarf, a heavy winter coat. I tugged on a pair of black rubber boots, the heels of which were worn and cracking. Assunta would remind me, and we would take the bus to find a cobbler to fix them. She would take me by the arm, and we would go as we pleased.

I walked through the house, snapping on lamps, then rested on the davenport, until once again I remembered Assunta.

The night was brisk, and the sky was crowded with new flakes of snow as I made my way carefully on the icy pavement to the backyard. My feet crunched on the path to the fence between our houses; I was glad for the dark, that no one could see me.

Assunta's house was pitch-black, except for a light around front in the utility room. I followed the light, bundling my coat to my chin. It seemed I had been out in the cold for hours. I could barely feel my feet. A little streak blared through the window, a bare bulb on a string. Peeking in, I saw only the washing machine and a few slips hanging across the line like silken ghosts. A chill ran through me.

Assunta's shoes were lying in the bright raw light, her feet a little splayed and wooden, perpendicular, as if nailed to the floor. They were a brown two-tone pair she had purchased on a trip to Toronto. I had always liked them. I tapped at the window. It was cold, and I liked a cup of coffee at night. It had been so many years since I had come to her doorstep, not since her parents were still alive; she ought, at least, to return the favor and let me in where it was warm.

The moon was indifferent, shining in the window as I stood there, tapping.

Assunta did not get up.

When I stood on my toes, I could see the top of her silvery head, but my view of her face was blocked by a metal locker. I tried to follow the tilt of her head and find her eyes, but the effort made my neck tight. I stopped my banging.

More snow fell, and I decided to go home.

The thought came to me out of nowhere, like nameless angels lighting. I made a hard little ball of snow from the ground near my feet and stood back a few steps from the window, struggling for space among the bushes. I hurled the little ball as hard as I could and waited for the sound of breaking glass to stop. Then I neared the open place in the window and spoke up as loudly as I could.

"How dare you?" I said. "*Regina, regina, regina.*"

The shrillness of my voice made me feel both happy and afraid; my heart raced. I could picture quite clearly how things would end, but it was not so much a surprise as a clear, calming thought. I kept watch as the ball of snow began to melt near Assunta's foot. From that room a warmth caressed my face, and I wanted to stay close, but the smell was overpowering; it moistened my eyes.

By the time I pulled myself from Assunta's window, a white sun had already overtaken the moon. My only concern was comfort: the ease of my bed, the scent of my kitchen, a welcoming friend. I tapped at my own back door, making a red smudge on the white paint and watching the blood from my hands make a curious pattern in the snow. I stood looking down at it, waiting. In just a few hours the young man would come and take my money to shovel it away.

Vanish

J ason lives and is getting ready to die in a six-story walk-up on
First Avenue and First Street. The doorways on his block and
beyond (from Third to B) look so much alike that often I worry
about the junkies and the predawn drunks finding their way
home. So much life crowded together makes a soul weary, and
after a while everything—even the blunt distinctions—gets lost.
A clutter of architecture and graffiti, a blur of noise and flesh:
There's only so much a person can take.

"*Kak tibya zavoot?*"

It is the Russian who stands outside the shoe repair on
Jason's block, asking my name in the familiar. Swaying in the
breeze, he smiles at me.

"What's it to you?" I reply meanly.

I have been mistaken for a Jew, a boy, a criminal, a prostitute, some lost child's mother, and now a Russian maiden. The grocery checkers call me "sir." But nobody mistakes me for who I am: "What are you, some kind of fool?" Or, now that it's chic to be gay, "Aren't you one of those lesbians?" Still, identity—mistaken or not—doesn't rankle far enough to touch me.

Nobody ever mistakes me for you, I've noticed. Nobody rushes up behind me, calling your name, grasping my hand, pushing their fingers through my hair. If I hadn't forgotten the exact shape of your face, the shade of your eyes, the taste of your skin, I would transform myself into you with a renewed hope of recognition.

But how likely is that? Since I stopped returning your calls, I've taken to insulting old men with the ripe indifference of a fourteen-year-old girl. Since shirking your life of daylight and work, I've led my own in wandering.

The thought of running into you makes me avoid corners, motors me forward at a fast clip. After work I have no choice but to cross town in daylight, but I am furtive, clocking my route. From my apartment on the West Side to the pharmacy for Jason's Seconal takes thirty-five minutes. The grocery where I pick up a few things for his dinner adds fifteen, more if the aisles are crowded with the homeless exchanging their empties for $1. Another step or two around the corner brings me to the shelter of Jason's doorway. Amidst the clutter and undistinguished architecture, his number is easy to spot, posted on either side by dull pink columns of stone that blend vaguely with the faded brick of his building. Once you see them, they are like signposts in the night's monotony.

There are few other distinguishing features on these streets save for the pigeons, remarkable in number and sheer audacity. The shopkeepers seem particularly generous with bread crumbs—either that or interested in goodwill and aviaries.

Pigeons are calm at sunset, fervent at midnight. In the mornings they murmur like insistent tender alarm clocks.

"How are you today, Jason?"

His apartment feels damp. A wall of cool bricks, painted white, at the far end keeps the heat down. On a good day he will get on his knees and scrub the kitchen tiles. "Does it smell like I'm dying in here?" he asks, particularly after someone has come for a visit, an old boyfriend or the delivery man.

I shake my head, a lie.

Today's question is the same as yesterday's, always the same. "How are you today, Jason?"

"Visionless," he says. He hasn't seen angels all week.

Jason is famous for his spiritual transformation, an ascent to the rafters that happened unexpectedly after a bout of shingles. At that time he was a teacher and a waiter with nothing remotely godlike up his sleeve. Now, like an uncalled-for miracle, his bed is surrounded by votive candles and the *Tao Te Ching*. He's not exactly famous, despite the sermons, the harmonic convergence, and the public television appearances. His world, after all, is precarious, a universe jerry-rigged by disease. But his name has a kind of currency in the new economy of HIV, and the story of his redemption is passed from person to person like a collection plate.

"They don't get it," Jason says, lamenting his comrades, the street activists, as he sulks over a bowl of chicken broth.

I too have come to eat only what his stomach can tolerate.

"Get what?" I say, watching my own soup grow cold.

"Spiritual salvation," he answers. "They need to make everything ugly. They need an enemy so bad that they turn against their own bodies. Then they turn against each other."

I imagine the virus as a disgusting infestation of killer flying bees or a filthy invasion of microscopic creatures, nesting just under the skin. Guilty, I try to change the direction of my thoughts, hoping he hasn't taken to reading minds.

Jason's eyes catch the last of the day's light—blue, when he is feeling well. I'm not sure I understand, but, as with all his lessons, I am patient.

"Well, not everyone can be a believer," I say, wiping my mouth. "Not everyone is a savior."

It's a stab in the dark; I watch to see how close I've come.

"Wrong!" Jason barks happily. "But exactly my point. Don't you see how they stomp around? Do you look in their eyes? They believe just precisely *that* with all their hearts. They *are* the new salvation. *Anyone* can be Jesus."

He leans back on his pillow, exhausted from dinner and his outburst. His index finger is still extended toward the ceiling.

I stare at him blankly.

"Don't you see?" he says quietly, trying again. "We have to be the ones to do what Jesus couldn't."

"What's that?" I am an ex-Catholic, within arm's length of blind faith and easy alarm. "What couldn't Jesus do? He raised the dead and loved his enemy. He delivered us from evil, for God's sake."

"Piece of cake." Jason is starting to sparkle again. "The hard part came when he was hanging there on the cross. He couldn't save himself, could he? He didn't even want to."

* * *

How long has it been? It was the week before Christmas when I stopped returning your phone calls. Somewhere near the first snow, I began the final preparations for the Vanish, feeling pleased with myself for stealing this trick from you, this particular kind of disappearing.

You used to tell me stories in bed about the lives you left behind in other women's apartments: stereo disc players, closets of clothes, tax records dating back to 1972. In an attic somewhere in Toledo sits an abandoned bed frame you once crafted by hand. In Orange County every last piece of your Polish grandmother's china remains carelessly behind with the only man who loved you. All of this was before you were a lesbian, before you were a prostitute, before you were a politician. In Duluth you unloaded a love seat and matching sofa while your unsuspecting sweetheart slept off a hangover during the first beams of morning. That time you slipped a note—crisp as a traffic ticket—under her windshield. The garbage men waved good-bye.

You were young then, a fugitive from nothing in particular, still imperfect at the art of escaping. The older you got, the less likely you were to leave fingerprints, though your moments of genius meant less to you than your mistakes, the times you almost got caught. Those you cherished, handled lovingly like simple-minded children, sitting in dark rooms turning each horrible detail over in your mind, polishing it smooth until it transformed itself from irritating piece of sand to gleaming hard pearl.

You made strings of tales for me to wear around my neck, and I did so willingly.

* * *

This year the street activists are slightly hungover, bloated from the long winter. They are young men in white socks and black boots, with full red lips that glisten when they speak of health. They are Jason's followers, ever on the prowl for a glimmer of hope. Despite their often unspoken status, they sport slim, tight bodies, more beautiful than any single woman I have ever laid hands on. They come to see for themselves how Jason has learned to outlive—through meditation and prayer—every bacteria and cancer, nearly without symptom. They recline by his side, captivated by Jason's luck, which they call his will.

I have seen it for myself. Jason's body does not respond as expected, and he seems to be a self-healer. Even the most vile drug infused through yellow tubing causes him only a week or so of napping or some minor difficulty with more complicated errands or trips out of town. Each time it is as if he has risen from the dead barely scathed.

"Immune tolerance," he announces one day after a quick struggle with mild PCP. He plops down a medical textbook in front of me on the table in a diner across from his apartment and orders a turkey dinner with cranberry sauce, as if it were Thanksgiving and he has received the gift of his former appetite.

"What?" I say, shifting in my booth, a place where I spend considerable hours trying to heal myself from the raw effects of obsessive love. I order mint tea as if I am the one who's been ill.

"It's the perpetual ability of a body to regain stasis and live no matter what has happened, is happening, or will happen to it," he reports.

He adds, to prove his point, "It is not just a philosophy but a little-known immunological fact."

I imagine scientists passing this theory around laboratories and cocktail parties, hoping such blasphemy won't spoil the opportunity to name an important disease molecule after themselves.

"The theory itself is older than medicine, proven by history and public health," Jason continues. "Living things change to accommodate life. If they are unable to, then they die. It's as simple as that."

"How long does it take?" I ask, vaguely calling up my memory of high school biology.

Jason shrugs, uninterested in mundane chronology.

But in my heart I know the answer: It takes time, a lot of time, more than even Jason's got.

By spring the activists begin to turn like spoiled milk, passing Jason's words around like rude, passionless kisses. They report on his immune tolerance, though they don't call it that. The ones who are less invested in cures respond with increasing ridicule. These are a small crowd of jaded young men, a handful of soap-scrubbed dykes. They run the general activist meetings every Monday night like clockwork. They facilitate each topic with a microphone and an amp, moving the conversation along like Nazis. When the discussion includes espionage, they worship the virus like a twelve-step obsession.

Others, unable to afford the cost of such cynicism, are more cautious.

"Jason Silverman outlived microsporidiosis by eating sushi and spending time with the gurus," one hopeful gay man says to the next. "Pass it on."

The summer of Jason's inevitable dying is when they all admit that, thirteen years later—an unlucky and not insignificant period of time—nobody knows anything. Not the scientists, not the politicians, not even the enemies.

"Finally," Jason says, approving the surrender, because he knows his own is imminent.

For the most part the whole crowd is growing restless, beginning to see at last that power is cheap and nothing is as it appears. The FBI isn't interested in phone-tapping anymore, and no one's being saved. The activists suddenly have little to do, now that there's no real direction, now that lying down in the street is passé. The money is running out. The young men are dying as fast as ever, adding to the ranks of the others: the women, the junkies, the poor sex-working lesbians, the incarcerated, the grandmothers, the shop owners. It is a whole city with AIDS.

Before long, no one seems to have the heart to recline by Jason's side. The activists see him around, though not at their meetings. Jason doesn't mind or even notice. He's moved on. He spends time at an ashram upstate and organizes on a completely different level.

* * *

"We are equals," you said the first time we met. "By the time we're through, you'll be more dangerous than I am."

You put it to me so simply, complete with a finite ending and a goal. It was difficult to resist. You seemed so sure of yourself, so sure of me. I had to know if I could do it, submerge myself in love without leaving a mark, want without needing. Somehow I thought I was ready for the challenge.

"You belong to me," you whispered in September.

Then, to my surprise, I found myself waiting for your Vanish. It would hit me at the strangest times—in the shower or while brushing my teeth. Countless nights I hoped to step out into the living room, dripping wet from the shower or ready for bed, to find you gone. But you were always there. We watched CNN in front of the TV you insisted on buying and keeping—still yours, of course—in my apartment. We tuned you in, interviewed on the late-night news. We applauded your brilliant political career and admired the Sony entertainment center for its electronic complexity. Meanwhile, I held my breath, braced for your inevitable and cruel exit. By the time December rolled around, I was beginning to catch on. Things were not going as you had originally promised.

How many times had you recounted in great detail that very first time you went airborne? I can still tell it by heart: A mere ringleted girl, you were barely thirteen, wrenching yourself free from a disappointing mother and her coterie of odd boyfriends who wanted to touch you when no one was looking. The mere act of catapulting is what thrilled you. You were completely unafraid, although eventually you would land somewhere in West Virginia and become a slave, prostitute, hippie. It was worth it, you said: all worth the freedom.

Still, as more snow fell, you lay in my arms and seemed to have forgotten the merits of flight.

* * *

The pigeons coo dreamily inside Jason's wall, inhabitants of a whole separate world. They nest inside, flapping with an intrigue and reason all their own.

Jason is the one who points them out. How they live their swollen lives tucked away behind the fridge and the stove. How they squeeze between the buildings to nap and preen. There are dozens of them. Each one is singular in its markings. Each one is crafty and suffering like a sly murderess.

"Maybe tomorrow they'll come," I say, meaning the angels.

But Jason is growing doubtful.

"I'm losing this battle to pigeons," he says.

He stands momentarily at the window on his way back from the bathroom. Hands on his hips, he exposes the blades of his shoulders, a few of his razor-sharp ribs, the surprising full moon of a hard white belly. He starts to believe that pigeons will be the death of him, having had his worst luck yet with this recent onset of cryptococcal meningitis. Cryptococcus is a disease of the brain that is, in fact, unearthed from moldy pigeon droppings, deadly to the immune-impaired who inhale. In a city with such a vast sweep of birds, it is nearly impossible to avoid exposure.

At night Jason finally rests after a few spoons of dinner. The headaches have passed, the medicine infused, and he dreams uneasily through a fever. A washcloth on his chest holds in the life-heat his body might otherwise expel.

"I've had a vision," he says between dozing.

"A vision of what?" I ask.

Our bodies are nearly touching in bed.

He doesn't answer right away.

"There isn't an enemy…" he says, his voice trailing off in a whisper. "Not even in dying."

He rolls on his side, away from me. It's late; our moods are unpredictable. The final word is his.

When he finally sleeps, I am roused by a thunderous flapping of wings. I sit for a while and listen to the rustling as if it were music. When I step out of bed, I am careful not to wake him. I feel my way in the dark across the apartment to the stove, cautious not to knock over the rows of Jason's medicine, vials and bottles lined up on every surface.

Behind the opaque glass of the window they watch me, dozens of button-size yellow-and-black eyes, peering steadily. When I flip on the bathroom light, they rush the window like giant moths.

"Stop," I whisper, tapping at the pane. "Go away."

They continue to butt at the glass, their heads the size of subway tokens. I pull up the window to shoo them off, throw my hands through the air. They take to me like crazed martyrs, impaling themselves on my fingers, scratching with orange toes. Some of them wear an iridescent shawl of green and purple; others are remarkably white, bloated and sick with begging. A wind shaft rushes them in all directions through the small crevice between Jason's building and the one next door. They mate for life, pigeons, and travel in extended families.

"Stupids!" I seethe, attacking them with a damp dishrag.

Finally, as if a message had been sent electronically from one to the next, they ascend like a dusty blanket into the sky. I take it as a sign and make my way silently down the five flights and out through the pink marble doorway. Unsteadied, I press my eyes to rub away their image. I step through the breezes like a sleepwalker shaking off a bad dream, pretending not to be searching for you, the one who, in the midst of losing so many, I willingly set free.

I loosen my joints, feeling connected to everything: the streetlights, the liquor stores, the Chinese laundry. The men in undershirts sit on their stoops, staring at yesterday's paper as if it were a movie. You'd never guess it was almost daybreak. The grates on the stores are locked tight against intruders. The fire hydrants let loose, spout water from the O's of their mouths. The calm blue glow of late-night TV escapes through various windows, and I am anything but lonely. All of this serves to remind me that in a city of eight million people, only one of them is you. The thought is both comforting and horrible.

* * *

What was there left for me to do that Christmas except prepare myself for flight? Reluctant to prove you right, I did just that. This time the Vanish was mine. It was easy, really: a simple change of apartments. My lease was up; I left a forwarding address just in case you wanted to pursue me.

But you had moved on to another lover, it turned out, long before I'd decided to go. I ought to have recognized the signs—the sudden lapsed hours, the smell of a new soap, the way you perched night after night on my Navajo pillows like the empty shell of an insect long gone but leaving a hollowed-out image to fool enemies, to throw me off. Now, however, in the middle of a New York night, even that seems irrelevant.

I have made my way across town and am heading up the street you live on between the Chelsea Hotel and the Associated Blind. I am standing next to your door when I spot you stepping out of a taxi. I want to turn around and say it's all a mistake, an insomniac's miscalculation, an error in navigation anyone could make. But you are dressed for some gala event, your face flushed. Perhaps you are running for office.

"How are you?" I say.

You don't seem surprised to see me. You pay the taxi with a twenty that you remove from a tiny black-pearled evening bag. It fits charmingly in the palm of your hand.

"I didn't exactly file a missing person's report on you," you say, "but I called a few times."

It's an apology of sorts.

"How's Betsy?" I inquire after your latest lover, someone I used to know before she dyed her hair jet-black and changed her name to something more dangerous.

"It's Bess," you correct. Your ire rises and falls like mercury.

We stand close under a streetlamp.

"You know what it's like," you continue intimately. "You never exactly plan to see each other again, but somehow you always do."

These lies are predictable, since you use people to fend off loneliness the way the rest of us use gravity to walk around the block. The grapevine is select in details: You're paying for a trip for two to Cozumel. In the meantime, Betsy/Bess has taken to the streets like a bully, plans on graduate school at your expense, and likes to press finger-size bruises into your arms like the fertile seeds of small budding flowers.

"Well," I say, my cue to move along.

"Well," you jump in, sounding like a matter-of-fact salesclerk. "You're awfully quick to forget what a good thing we had. You used to say we had a great love."

I shrug, unable to move anything but my shoulders, which have come unhinged. I am still slightly buzzed by the realization that you make yourself up from scratch each day: a loner, a cowgirl, a spy. The look you give me rouses my sex like Lazarus. Coyly you pull me close and put your mouth on mine. Long, slow, and hard, you unravel me. Time merges like rush-hour traffic, and suddenly I am traveling through you. As if in a movie, I remember why it is my character fell in love with yours in the first scene. It gave me a purpose better than salvation; it secured my survival as the hero of the story. A good enemy, after all, is the essence of self-definition.

I pull away and stare at my feet, toying with the idea of dropping to my hands and rubbing my face against the sidewalk. Perhaps it isn't true love unless you leave a small mark on someone's tender flesh. Maybe the flesh ought to be mine, the mark a sign that I remember love at all.

"We could have it again," you offer, always one to hedge a bet, to trade a something for a nothing.

Only you would be glib in the language of loss.

Why does no one cherish innocence? You'll never know how brief mine was, what a flash of light, irrevocable as birth, a gift, a slamming door. Sometimes I miss the days when I ignored pigeons, worshiped at the temple of danger, and drank you in like a saltwater lake. Now I have soothed the dying, and there's no way back. Now I'm left to wonder if destructive love was just a dress rehearsal for death, a way to pass the time. Why did I fall in love with you? Holding the weight of a truth and a lie in my arms, I cannot tell them apart.

* * *

By the time I look up, you are gone. Still, the memory of you has diminished to a human proportion. I begin to wind my way back to Jason's.

Usually I find him half awake, restless, miserable. Those times there is nothing to do but rub his spine, purple and bruised by the needles, as he whimpers, "Help me."

Today I rush to the corner, hoping he'll be awake when I get there so I can tell him this final story of you. But, standing with my key in the door of his building, I hesitate, seeing his angels at last.

I let them drift by: the small parade of lost souls, angry activists, vanished loves. Ghostlike and silent, they skulk by like the ones who did us wrong, the ones we destroyed. In the end they are the ones who really suffered—missing persons and East Village dwellers, hollowed-out shells of activists who believed that the government was trying to murder them, and who can say it isn't true?

When I enter Jason's apartment, it is drafty. The ceiling fan is not running, but the window is spinning out dirty breezes. I shut it quietly and follow a faint trail of soot to the edge of Jason's bed where I see everything so clearly. The distinctions, all together in a blur, snap temporarily into focus. No signs of life except pigeon feathers, hundreds of them everywhere.

"They have come," I whisper, as if I have known all along who Jason's angels would turn out to be.

The frothy scent of redemption is rising.

And who was saved? I hear him say, ever the teacher.

"The ones who suffered," I say, since I have known them well.

And who are they? he asks to make sure I understand the question.

I point to Jason's family, the desperate souls crowding his doorway, who have marched in protest, loved in vain, organized absently, rehearsed their whole lives for moments like this and still refuse to belong. I watch them as they begin to fade.

"Us," I say, though now I know there is no such thing.

Accidents

They have me walk the halls at night to keep me going. That's what the doctors say—to keep my mind moving, my body in shape. The nuns are afraid to leave me in my room after dark, afraid of what I might do. I follow their orders, walking the different wards like a nomad, marking my surroundings, preferring the women's division, which is closest to home. Painted green and slightly sanitary, the whole east wing appears to be submerged in deep, cleansing waters. I try not to limit myself according to the color of walls but branch out instead, shuffling in the paper slippers that arrive every morning sealed in plastic Baggies. At St. Mary's Hospital and Rehabilitation Center, life is airtight.

When I get tired of walking, I ride the elevator, never stepping off on any floor. Listening to the music is good for my spirits; I pretend that riding up and down stirs up a breeze against the staleness, a kind of public service for the paralyzed, the bedridden. None of the windows actually opens, but if you're determined, you can stand on a chair and slide the top pane over just enough to stick out your face. Chairs for this feat are hard to locate, unless you can manage on wheels.

Every once in a while there's a little excitement on one of the wards. Usually something strays out of place: A rolled-up pair of socks wanders to the water fountain; an open cup of chocolate pudding is spotted at the north wing utility basin. Because the nuns run a pretty tight ship, events as minor as these take on an air of mystery, suggesting foul play, though to my knowledge, no one's ever been fired.

Mother Superior expects all sorts of mistakes: She doesn't believe a person can ever achieve perfection. I've noticed too that few things seem to faze her. Once, when a new arrival to the quadriplegic ward suffered a heart attack during afternoon rounds, Mother Superior applied CPR without batting an eyelash. As close to God as they come, she seems to have insights into his mysteries. Often I am surprised by her gum-chewing at the east-wing station. I stumble across her imposing figure, hands on hips, exasperated by some inept doctor's orders, as if she were not God's servant at all.

The strange little incidents in the ward where I am stationed occur infrequently and cause little disruption in the daily business of healing the sick, although they tend to startle the daytime nursing staff, common nuns in sensible shoes who pull at their habits and stand around looking quizzical.

"Someone's feet got hot?" they say. Or later, after some thought, snapping their fingers: "One of the night sisters is diabetic!"

For the most part these strange phenomena offer the staff a whole new topic of conversation. It's nice to have a mystery to solve.

Keeping track of the hospital's goings-on, I write down my careful observations on a pad of white paper with a stubby yellow pencil I found one night stuck behind a hand dryer in the lobby rest room. It seemed like a sign. As a rule I keep my notes short and to the point and try not to make them seem like complaints, but rather memoranda. I don't like to keep people from their work, but I do get lonely for Anabel, and things occasionally need fixing. In the morning I bring my nightly travelogue to the most senior person in charge, who is always Mother Superior.

I am vigilant with my note-taking: Once a stack of year-old newspapers appeared by the freight elevator. Another time it was a pile of empty egg cartons, which had materialized in the chapel; they found them at vespers dripping egg yolk on the altar. And just the other week, stray surgical gloves were found stuffed under every mattress in the ward.

As if on my behalf, the day staff grows more creative with solutions.

"A protest against recycling laws?" Sister Mary Claude suggests.

She brings the newspapers herself to the elementary school, where they will use a little origami trick she learned at the convent and some gold spray paint to make Christmas trees.

"Someone's making protein shakes," whispers Josephine knowingly. "Probably it's the Dislocated Hip on Women's Ward East. I saw her reading *Dianetics*." Josephine is not a nun but reads the Bible daily, a distinction that allows her to be a bit less pious than the others.

"Perhaps it's some sort of satanic cult," Sister Theresa hisses excitedly over Josephine's birdlike shoulder. They stand together like the twins of mischief, pale and nunlike, at the end of my bed.

"But wouldn't they sacrifice the chicken first?" I scribble.

Sister Theresa, who is a large woman, laughs boisterously, not like you might expect from a nun. A patient across the hall coughs in response, and someone shuts a door. Sister Theresa quiets, letting her reading glasses slip from her nose to a dangling position around her neck. She presses my note discreetly inside her habit, no doubt to use at the afternoon staff meeting as evidence of my good spirits.

"I think someone around here is getting better," she says, patting my hand.

I like to make the sisters laugh. I devise new and clever ways to be charming. It is remarkable, their carefree joy, never a single trace of remorse or slip of pain in their eyes. I know; I have looked.

"A crime is being planned!" I hear them whispering in the hallways the day following the surgical gloves episode. I wonder if they do it to cheer me up, an attempt to distract. Or perhaps they hope to ease my sorrow and lift my tongue again with prayer.

After the accident someone actually managed to stitch my tongue back on. This is a miracle—that's what everybody says. I am told quite regularly how lucky I am. My jaw is immovable, wired shut, but I can still feel my tongue lying like a piece of meat at the bottom of my mouth, making me try to sense what "lucky" feels like. I aim for an exact approximation of fortune. Some day soon, I tell myself, the conversations I long for will tie up my days and nights. I will chat easily with the weekend janitor, who is also a deacon for the chapel. I will joke with the Catholic volunteer who collects my daily menu.

Asking the right question at the right time, I will also solve all the mysteries of St. Mary's myself. Then Mother Superior will forgive my sins, for she is the highest authority around.

For now, this ward has become my home. I am comfortable here, except for my tongue, which twitches nervously behind my teeth. The doctors say I'm making progress. They are pleased with my nightly excursions, amazed that I can walk at all. Soon I will have to practice opening my mouth, which now happens only when they come along with their penlights to unhook the wires and have a look.

No one likes it when the doctors come; their bossiness interrupts the peaceful flow. I say "A-a-ah" when they tell me to, but I don't really mean it. I sympathize too much with the nuns. They are the ones who really run the place. I have come to adore them, their comforting white-and-black uniforms, their quiet smiles offered no matter what. They know about my accident and do not judge. Even the unpleasant ones are pleasant in their way.

Anyone who walks these lonely halls when most patients are asleep can't help but discover the secret ritual: The nuns do laundry at night to preserve hot water for our afternoon showers. Carts of fresh sheets and towels litter the vast corridors until 10 p.m., when they are momentarily pushed aside to make way for the floor-polishing machine. Also driven by a nun, it comforts with its nearly silent purr.

The other nuns tiptoe in pairs, folding the linens: They stand far apart from one another, the distance of a perfect white rectangle, one on either side, and silently toss a blanket or sheet out between them to shake out the wrinkles. Then they begin their easy movements—together and then apart in smaller and smaller intervals until each sheet and blanket is ready for storage. I follow their work closely, watching the sheets fall like snow and harden into perfectly stacked piles.

It chills me to the bone, just as if the sky from that very night had opened up, leaving me a blanket of pure white to remind me.

It happened like this.

I met Carter on the corner close to his house. It was one of those amazing frozen nights that hung in the air like an icicle, and the stillness startled me. No one was out shoveling their driveways that night, when Alan took Anabel to Michigan to stay with my mother while we figured things out. The place seemed deserted, so I emptied my mind: Even the most inhumane problems seemed capable of being tucked away, stuffed into a freezer like a neat package of meat.

My mother's house was the only answer I could think of for Anabel: For days she wouldn't speak, sobbing, refusing even her favorite food. We put her at the kitchen table, bought cartons of crayons to distract her, but her pictures were startling, dark scribbles of men. They made her vomit. The baby-sitter's older brother, she said, and another family friend. Alan and I were devastated. What did we know? We'd never left her alone with strangers. Suddenly, though, the distinction between knowing a person and not knowing a person didn't seem so clear.

Everything was still the night I walked toward Carter: Only the streetlights buzzed against a crisp yellow moon, vying for attention. From a distance I could see Carter in the driver's seat, leaning toward the dashboard. He looked the same as he always did, which surprised me a little. I was aware of feeling disappointed, as if he ought to seem better than usual, as if my idea to escape reality ought to have had a greater impact on him.

Carter had called around 10 p.m., after I returned from the airport. I had sat in my car in the short-term-parking lot, waiting until their plane was safely in the air. It's not the thing a mother should say, but I suddenly felt free, as if a heavy burden had been lifted, flying over my head with all its metal and diesel, leaving me momentarily carefree. I waved up at the sky through the windshield at Alan and Anabel, who could no longer see me. I waved good-bye to my Anabel, feeling exonerated, feeling that he could take care of things for a while, until my mother took over.

After I witnessed the plane's taking off, I returned home and wasn't in the door twenty seconds when the phone rang and it was Carter asking if they'd gotten off okay. There was nothing new to report: They'd gotten off fine, but I felt desperate in the house without her—something about it felt wrong. I had thrown away all of her terrible drawings, but they still haunted me. *How could I not have known?* That was really what I was thinking when I first got the idea about Carter. He was completely familiar, but suddenly the thought of him seemed new.

"How about a drive?" I asked him, pushing my plan into motion.

He answered by not saying anything.

"Pick me up on the corner," I said, then hung up.

I had known Carter longer than I'd known Alan. They were best friends since childhood, but Carter and I went to college together. We shared the first letter of our last names and so were seated in every class a few chairs from each other near the other ends of the alphabet. Carter was the one who introduced Alan to me one summer. Alan was still in architecture school. He was handsome, able to engage both Carter and me without making either of us jealous.

Carter stood up at our wedding and made a beautiful toast.

When it was time to have Anabel, Carter was the one willing to drive me to the hospital through the worst snowstorm of the decade.

Before that night, before that very instant, when the phone rang and it was Carter on the other line, it had never occurred to me to go to bed with him. He was Anabel's godfather, her favorite grown-up. The very thought seemed almost obscene.

But as I drew closer to the designated corner, I could make out Carter's slightly apologetic form against the shadows. The cigarette he was lighting glowed imperfectly against the windshield, a flash of orange glimmer that was inadequate to light our way. We had known each other now for so many years that we were long beyond the need for such markers, off the guided path, so to speak. I slid into the passenger seat of Carter's Volkswagen, and we started out, winging through the neighborhood at 11 p.m. like thieves in the night, though at that point it was hard to know the object of our pilfering, what it was we were actually getting away with.

"Where should we go?" Carter said, stopping for gas at a 7-Eleven.

I remember his voice, how it rose above the radio, slightly strained, the way a man always sounds before he thinks he's going to get laid. His blond head almost touched the ceiling of the car. But still, he seemed a little lost in the familiar blue parka, armed against the weather as if it were the only enemy.

I struggled for an answer, knowing what I knew.

"Just drive," I said, pretending to be the kind of person whose life always works out in the end.

Carter drove us to Hunter Mountain. The winding road on the other side was where we were headed. I liked the names of the ski trails there because Alan and I had been to the Big

Apple on several occasions: The beginners' trail was named
The BMT, a subway line; the intermediate trail was named
Wall Street; and then there were the advanced slopes, Belt
Parkway and Central Park West. The latter two were Alan's
favorites; he was the real athlete. I just went along for the hot
toddies and the comforts of the lodge. That night I was in the
mood for the irony, I guess. Somehow those slopes reminded
me of how huge the gap between me and the rest of the world
was. A near-midnight drive through the mountains was as
ridiculous as a ski slope named New York City.

We had been driving for quite a while when I moved my hand
through the dark to locate Carter's fly. As I unzipped him, I
could not help wondering if those men made Anabel touch
them too. How do things like that happen? I unfastened the
button on Carter's pants and was trying to free him as he grew
hard, but his penis was tangled in his briefs. We were both
completely wordless, and I could hear his familiar breath getting thick in his throat, a sound I had never heard from him
before. It was surreal. The road was dark, and there were no
other cars in sight. We were sort of suspended in time and
space. That's how it felt, anyway, and it was nice to be without the context. I unsnapped my seat belt but still could not
fully reach him.

"Take it out," I whispered.

Lifting himself from the seat slightly, Carter pulled down
his jeans. I eagerly took hold of him and began to stroke. I
heard myself cooing as if he were a baby. The words felt
strange, like oddly shaped teeth coming loose in my mouth.
Carter said nothing but groaned, and I sped up my motions,
then slowed them down, an old front-seat trick I'd learned
when I was still in high school, long before I'd ever heard of
Carter or Alan. I didn't want to think about it. Carter felt tal-

cumy and smooth in my fingers. His penis was thin and bowed up at the end, all of which I could tell through touch, a faculty that had been sharpened by the darkness around us and the fact that we were going nowhere in particular.

He came almost immediately. Maybe it was the excitement of having his best friend's wife touch him like that. Maybe he had been secretly in love with me all these years and never uttered a word. Maybe it was just that we had known each other for so long and had never crossed the line before. I couldn't decide whether it was romantic or insulting. I held the wheel while he cleaned himself up with a Kleenex, my eyes on the road, guiding the car forward perfectly in a straight line. That part was without incident. The night seemed to stretch out perfectly and crisp without a single obstacle in sight.

Carter resumed control of the wheel, trying to smile reassuringly at me. At first we didn't see the other car, not even after Carter was tucked back in, his seat belt on. It was as if he had his eyes in the right direction, but his mind was somewhere else. He never even flinched. I was busy trying to refasten my own seat belt, thinking out loud about letting Anabel go to school in Michigan for the rest of the school year, when his body stiffened and I realized something was terribly wrong. Before I could get my seat belt on, Carter stepped on the brake and threw his arm across to the passenger's side. The back of his hand slapping my face shocked me more than the headlights flashing in my eyes, two white psychedelic flowers coming at me in slow motion.

Strangely, I didn't feel anything but a lack of gravity: Lifting off, I could see my hair, which must have come free from the braid, and there was a loud sound in my ears. I think it must have been the screeching wheels or the sound of someone screaming; it was unidentifiable, like Anabel's crying after hours and hours of labor. I hadn't had any idea what all the racket was then either.

I touched the top of Carter's car with my head. Inexplicably, I was at the passenger window, looking out. It was beautiful, really, as if I were underwater, somehow involved in an amazingly well-choreographed water ballet, both graceful and empty, a sea creature about to break the surface. The arc my body made sent me precisely through the windshield and out into the dark night, which stung my lungs like a slap of ice-cold water.

In one way, it was glorious to move like that, a fragile trajectory of skin and bone. In another way, it wasn't me at all; I was thinner than air, already in the process of disappearing from the elements, water and atmosphere, which were now in a jumble. I was nearly a nonentity, projecting unmistakably toward heaven, my ghosting touched into motion by forces I did not truly understand. Still, the whole thing seemed somehow familiar, as if I had been through it before.

Later, on my back, watching the sky, I was amazed at the vastness of the celestial bodies and knew that I had momentarily become one. My head ached, and I began to count and name the constellations with uncanny precision; it eased the pain. The bitter taste in my mouth reminded me of a hangover, the way gin and tonic tastes the morning after. I tried to call out for Anabel, but my tongue, which I remembered biting as I hit the pavement, was nowhere to be found.

There, lying on my back, somewhere on a dark road miles away from anything, I remembered the look on Anabel's face: It was as if a million chimes had been set off, ringing in my ears. That's when I knew that everything was a lie. That's when I knew that Anabel was one of those dark children, throwing unexplained fits, hiding her face when company came, crawling into her daddy's lap for comfort but shrinking at his touch. How I had never noticed before, I do not know.

After that, things went blank.

The mind is a tricky place, that's what people say. Mine, in particular, seems filled with bad neighborhoods where it's unsafe to stray, especially at night. That's why I prefer my sojourns through the hospital. "Never travel alone," my mother used to warn us when we were kids growing up in Michigan on the edge of Black Lake. "Don't talk to strange men." That was a long time ago, when danger was confined to the woods or dark movie theaters, to men who wanted to touch you precisely because you were someone else's daughter. In a million years we could never have guessed all the ways in which our mothers were mistaken.

I concentrate on mental exercises, reconstructing my own ancient school photographs, water-stained now and tucked away in my mother's basement, circa 1962. I conjure up a neat arrangement of brightly dressed children smiling for the camera. I visualize each class, picking them out, the ones who returned damaged from the zoo and the other long car rides with their own fathers. I name them all, misfits who crowd into the corner of the classroom, covering their eyes with locks of hair pulled intentionally out of place. They dot the landscape of the other pretty smiling children, threatening to pull apart my happy dream of a happy family. Like my Anabel once she turned seven, these children never smiled.

When I awoke in the hospital, Carter was there. His was the first face that came into focus. I tried to smile and say something but could make only the noise of a small animal getting caught in the spokes of a bicycle wheel. Carter put his finger in front of his lips and blew a little warm air on my face to quiet me down. But it went on, the sounds ripping me open and tearing at the stitches. In response, the gentle nuns came to check on me, at first without saying a word. I noticed how they seemed to list, as if dancing to the sound of my grief.

For weeks consciousness fluttered over me like a giant eyelid. I lost track of everything. One time I woke and saw Anabel, like an angel, sitting before me. She was reaching out to me or over me, wearing a white lace party dress, her hair neatly curled in pretty tendrils. She was asking for something, but I didn't know what. In her hands she gripped a few bright sticks of crayon, only they were broken where the paper had been peeled away. It looked like she had gnawed at them, as if she could take it all back by devouring the crayons.

Carter is the one who tells me what I already know.

"They never showed up in Michigan, Kat," he says, apparently astounded, thinking I will be as surprised as he is. "They disappeared."

Sometimes when I wake up, Alan—or my dream of him—is hovering nearby, cracking his knuckles and clearing his throat. I see his hand on her red princess cape, his fingers resting on her torso, blotting over the smooth velvet as he pulls her closer. Her head comes exactly to his belt buckle. She smiles and waves good-bye. I can smell the airport.

I try to dream only of Anabel, to open my eyes and catch her there, to reach my hand out for her tiny hand. The nighttime nuns interrupt their nightly laundry to come and sit with me.

"Don't call for her, dear," they say, kindly. "God's watching out for her now. And you'll only rip the stitches."

Nuns seem instinctively to understand a mother's love, as if it somehow equals their love for Jesus or maybe their love for all the poor paralyzed souls who pass through these doors. I wonder irreverently if any of them have ever been pregnant or given unsanctified birth. But I end up deciding that in the universe of God's servants, intrigue is unlikely: Instead, word travels fast, and sympathy abounds.

I have played it hundreds and hundreds of times, digging for answers, as if something obvious has simply been missed, but my time for missing details has long since passed. We still deploy search parties, put out APBs, run Anabel's picture on milk cartons. It seems unreal, like a made-for-TV movie. I am the actress, waving at the airport to her daughter and husband, tragically believing that everything is fine. Despite the psychiatrist they send me every Tuesday, I am not crazy. I sat there in my car watching that plane take off for Michigan, fully present, the way I always am: alert and confident. I couldn't have known that I had long since become Alan's fool, that my life with him was a game. This is no excuse, I know; I am the first to admit that no matter what, I am still the fool. You can ask me all you want, but I can't tell you a thing.

No one really believes in accidents anyway—not the kind that are pure chance, sheer misfortune; they're out of fashion. Someone is always standing nearby ready to interpret or offer an explanation, as if everyone had agreed to agree: Happenstance is out-of-date. Maybe the world has grown too complicated. Maybe we are too smart for our own good, blaming fate, blessings, divine will, repression. Carter and the other driver walked away from the wreck, but I am Anabel's mother. I should have known.

I've seen the women on *Oprah* and *Sally Jessy Raphaël*. I have watched them during the day, how guiltily they answer questions. They may refuse to believe it, refuse to turn in the guilty party, but none of them seems surprised. I guess a person's whole life can become a kind of secret she keeps from herself, a way to maintain the necessary forward motion.

Some secrets and some lives are simply more terrible than others. I watch the women high above my ahead on the hospital television, affixed to the opposite wall, unable to tear my eyes away. I watch as if it were a public execution, and I am next in line for hanging.

During a commercial break, Mother Superior makes her visits.

"I've been looking for you," she says, as if I am not easy to locate.

I click off the television and glance around my room, shrugging.

"I think we need to talk," she says patiently.

I comply with her tone, reaching for my notepad, which I've taken to wearing around my neck on a string.

"There's something you need to know," the Mother begins.

I wait expectantly, like a child who has been called to the principal's office, awaiting either punishment or praise, but not sure which. Despite her age, Mother Superior's skin seems cleared away of wrinkles. Perhaps she wears a bit of makeup. Her cheeks seem unnaturally rosy.

"Kathryn," she says, "terrible things happen, and we all have to accept that fact, but it doesn't mean you should give up. What would Anabel think?"

She says it slowly and evenly, looking all the time into my eyes, as if at any moment something might occur there.

"If you spend your time trying to understand evil, you'll be lost, Kathryn."

That is all. She pauses, sizing me up.

"But what about God?" I write.

"It's the same predicament: There's no contest when it comes to good against evil. Evil always wins, Kathryn; that's why God refuses to play."

Mother Superior smiles at me.

"What about forgiveness?" I write, my letters desperate and loopy.

She takes a minute to read and then consider my question.

"Evil is unforgivable," she says.

The pencil in my hand begins to quiver. Abruptly she catches my hand to hold it still.

"Will Anabel ever forgive me?" I write.

Mother Superior is tall from the waist up, although her legs seem a bit short and muscled for the rest of her. She bends a little when she speaks, perhaps because her voice never rises above the sound of someone humming quietly to herself.

"Probably not," she says. "But, Kathryn, you have to forgive yourself."

Sometimes, around evening, I stretch my legs to get a little head start on my nightly sojourns. I walk to the north-hall window bank and watch as Mother Superior strolls through the parking lot in her sneakers. Her calf muscles flex a little with each bouncing step. Disguised in a heavy winter coat and muffler, she locates her Toyota Corolla and slides in to the driver's seat, as if she's off to the supermarket or mall like any other regular person.

"Now," she says abruptly, "how about an end to the mysteries of St. Mary's? I think the sisters have had about as much excitement as they can take with all these strange little accidents. Mary Claude is calling for an exorcist."

I eye the mother a bit suspiciously, sizing her up as she stands rocking on her heels.

"I trust you know to what I am referring."

Some part of me doesn't want to admit I know what she means, but another part feels relieved.

Yes, Mother, I want to say, reverently nodding my head.

There are no more mysteries to report during my nightly excursions. The fact comes as a bit of a surprise, and sometimes I still catch myself looking for trouble. I spend most of my time writing letters to anyone who may help me while I wait for winter to turn to spring. Only God is with me now, here in the corridors of St. Mary's Hospital and Physical Rehabilitation Center. I know because I never let myself surrender completely.

According to the frosty glass of the hospital panes, it is still cold outside. Sometimes I balance on wheelchairs to open up the window tops and let in a little fresh air. I imagine myself calling out to Mother Superior on her bouncy way through the parking lot, as if she is any other mother in any other parking lot in town, but I don't know what it is I'd like to say. I write myself notes but try not to litter.

Last night on the ward, someone tried to kill herself, a woman with legs paralyzed from an accident of her own. She used razors on her thighs in order not to feel the pain. The nighttime nuns fill me in, smiling sympathetically over their laundry, as if the world made sense.

"I'll look out for her," I write, knowing that I will be the kind of friend who offers no interpretation. Maybe by the time she gains consciousness, I'll have recovered my tongue; I'm scheduled on Monday to meet with a new speech pathologist, a nun from another order.

I don't give myself much more hope than that: a paralyzed friend, a conversation, and prayers for Anabel.

The other night, though, I had a dream, my first real one since arriving at St. Mary's; it came in the morning, just before dawn. In it, everything was melting, and I realized that spring had finally come: a relief, a change in the weather. Watching nature transform herself into a new season, I began to hope for all kinds of things: Anabel's return, a bright future. But when I went to report it to the day staff, already bright and cheery, consumed by the day's work ahead, the feeling evaporated; I realized I had nothing to say. Instead, I walked to the east wing and left my message taped to the window, facing out toward a row of parked cars and a dirty pile of snow.

"There is no winter at St. Mary's Rehabilitation," the note said. Underneath those words was just enough space for someone guilty to sign her name.

Acknowledgments

I am deeply indebted and devoted to Alba Susana Lopez Johnson, to whom I dedicate this book and my love, and to Luna, who keeps me company during the day when all the exciting things happen.

Helen Eisenbach is a remarkable editor, whose generosity and intelligence I am lucky to receive; she called me on her first day at Alyson and continued to encourage me throughout the grueling process of my own imagination. The titles "Nuclear Family," "Practical Anthropology," and "Still Life" are Helen's brainchildren; "Consecration" would not exist if she hadn't pushed me to tell that particular story.

Instrumental to my completing this collection is the Tuesday Night Women's Writing Group: Risa Denenberg,

Acknowledgments

Evan Harris, and Cara Palladino, comrades in arms, literary devotees, and great cooks, all three.

Gerry Gomez Pearlberg edited some early drafts, invited me to read at Dixon Place, and ever gently reminded me that writing is about art, not money; Evan Harris never once got tired of sharing the daily writerly turmoil in a thousand and one phone calls made and received.

Thank God for Joan Nestle, who chose an earlier version of "Vanish" to launch my fiction (at last) into print; her commitment to emerging lesbian writers is fortifying.

These stories tell a metaphorical truth, not a literal one; I do not aim to make personal statements, pass secret judgments, or encode cryptic messages to the dozens of people (friends, acquaintances, and family members) from whom I have randomly borrowed life—everything from hair color to hobby to traumatic transforming events, to pets, to names and places of birth. I used other people's details only to write myself into these stories and (I hope) to make them sing: Thank you for the loan, but don't read too deeply for hidden meanings—it really is meant to be fiction.

The following people, in particular, have helped shape this collection with technical advice, moral support, and general inspiration without probably even trying: Christopher Canatsey, Sally Cooper, Beverly Coyle, the entire Crooker family, Alexis Danzig, David Freudenthal, Jon Greenberg (who died in July 1994), Jill Fischer, Eamon Grennan, Ann Imbrie, Wayne Kawadler, Eric Lee, Sharon Lerner, Helen Lang and Carole Maso (who graced me with a Cummington Community of the Arts Writer's Residency in 1988 to work on my still-in-progress novel), Griffin Meyer, Jennifer Milici, Rebecca Moore, Carolyn Patierno (the original mean Italian girl whom I love forever), Paula Pressley, Paul Russell, Martha Rosas, David Roche (who died in February 1994), and Jennifer Rudolph Walsh.

Charlotte Sheedy and Neeti Madan continue to encourage and advise in their ever straightforward and comforting manner.

Without the expertise and steady calm of Dixie Coates Beckham, I would never have found the confidence to recognize the truth in a single story, let alone my own.

Finally, I hope to make proud the many brave survivors I've had the privilege to know and learn from; their names are always with me.